ALFIE THE WEREWOLF

Full Moon

Written by

Paul van Loon

Translated by

David Colmer

Illustrated by

Hugo van Look

Hodder
Children's
Books

A division of Hachette Children's Books

Copyright © 1999 Paul van Loon
Illustrations copyright © 1999 Hugo van Look
English language translation © 2010 David Colmer

First published in The Netherlands under the title *Volle Maan*
by Uitgeverij Leopold in 1999
Published by arrangement with Rights People, London

First published in Great Britain in 2010 by Hodder Children's Books

The right of Paul van Loon and Hugo van Look to be identified as the
Author and Illustrator of the Work has been asserted by them in accordance
with the Copyright, Designs and Patents Act 1988

The publishers are grateful for the support of the Foundation
for the Production and Translation of Dutch Literature.

1

A Catalogue record for this book is available from the British Library

ISBN 978 0 340 98979 1

Typeset in Weiss by Avon DataSet Ltd,
Bidford on Avon, Warwickshire

Printed and bound in Great Britain by
Bookmarque Ltd, Croydon, Surrey

The paper and board used in this paperback by Hodder Children's Books
are natural recyclable products made from wood grown in
sustainable forests. The manufacturing processes conform to the
environmental regulations of the country of origin.

Hodder Children's Books
a division of Hachette Children's Books
338 Euston Road, London NW1 3BH
An Hachette UK Company
www.hachette.co.uk

1

Run!

'You, stop!'

Alfie Span didn't stop and he didn't look back at the man who was chasing him in the dark on a motorbike. He kept running as fast as he could. The man had a big head of bushy hair and a big moustache and he was wearing a big leather coat. He roared over the pavements and swerved between the parked cars, the beam of his headlight zigzagging across the street.

Alfie shot from left to right, but the light kept following him. His heart was pounding in his chest. His tongue was hanging out of his mouth.

'Tired, eh?' the man yelled. 'I'll get you!'

But Alfie ducked out of the way and hid in the shadows. Panting, he looked from left to right. Where could he go? He was worn out and his stomach was full because he'd just stuffed himself. That was why he couldn't run fast enough. He looked up at the full moon in desperation, and immediately stepped in a puddle, splashing water up into his eyes.

'I'll get you, yes, you horrible hen hunter,' the man shouted behind him.

The moon disappeared behind a black cloud. Rain pattered down on the roofs of the cars and the street turned gleaming black. The next thing Alfie knew, a bright light was glaring in his eyes. He flinched and covered his face.

'I've got you now!' he heard.

Alfie saw a black silhouette on a motorbike.

The man jerked the handlebars, making the motorbike rear up like a horse. Then he pulled a club out from under his coat. Alfie looked around and shrank. There was nowhere to run. The motorbike towered over him as the man swung the club over his head. Things were looking bad for Alfie, but that was just for a second.

The rain had made the road so slippery that the back wheel slid. The motorbike skidded and fell, sending the man rolling over the road and the club bouncing on to the pavement. The back wheel screeched as it spun around in the air.

For a moment Alfie stood there gaping. He could hardly believe he'd escaped.

'Run, you idiot!' he growled to himself.

He glanced back one last time at the furious man, who was picking himself up, then ran off on all fours, as fast as he could.

'Eh, stop, you nasty little wolf.'

The roar of the motorbike started up again as Alfie ran around a corner. Someone grabbed him. Two hands pushed him to the ground. Something came down on top of him.

2

Deaf?

'Quick, get up and put this coat on fast,' a voice hissed. Alfie's heart leapt.

'Tim! What are you doing here? I—'

'No time.' Tim sounded hurried. 'Stand on your hind legs. Stick your forepaws in the sleeves, quick.'

He helped Alfie into the long raincoat as the roar of the motorbike came closer. Tim pulled a baseball cap down over Alfie's head and wrapped a scarf around his neck and chin, so that only his glasses were visible. The rain was still beating down. Water was dripping off of Alfie's tail, which was sticking out slightly under the coat. Tim's hair was sopping wet too.

'Come on, let's get home,' he said.

A beam of white light swept over them and the throbbing motorbike stopped just in front of them.

'Eh, boys, wait a sec, eh?'

Tim held up one hand to keep the bright light out of his eyes. Alfie stayed as quiet as

a mouse and looked the other way. The man on the motorbike wiped his nose with his arm and sniffed loudly.

'Did you see a wolf run past here? A little white one, eh? With glasses.'

Tim cocked an eyebrow and twisted his face into a crooked grin. 'A wolf with glasses, you say?' He snorted with exaggerated laughter.

'There's no need to laugh at me, eh?' the man growled. 'There was a white wolf in my henhouse. It was wearing glasses! And it ate one of my hens. A nice fat one, eh?'

'A fat white wolf with glasses?' Tim asked.

'No, a fat hen. I was going to eat it myself for Christmas, eh?'

The headlight was still shining on Tim and Alfie. The man studied them and sniffed again. Rainwater dripped from his moustache.

'Maybe your friend saw something, eh?' he asked.

Alfie didn't say a word. His glasses were covered with raindrops but he was too scared to wipe the lenses. He hoped the man wouldn't look down at his feet.

The man peered at him. 'What are you being so quiet about, eh?' He got off his motorbike. 'I asked you something, pea-brain. You deaf or what? Show your face, eh?' He lunged at the scarf. Alfie shrank back.

'No . . .'

3

Best Friends

Quickly Tim moved over in front of Alfie.

'Oh,' he exclaimed. 'Now I remember. I did see something white run past a minute ago.' He pointed. 'Over there, on the other side of the street. I thought it was a dog or something.'

'That was it!' the man shouted. 'Not a dog or something, a wolf! You should have told me at once, eh? Stupid brat! If it gets away, it's your fault.'

The man jumped on his motorbike, muttered something to himself and shot off down the street and into the darkness. The roar of the motor died away in the distance. Tim looked at Alfie.

'Phew, that was close. What a bully.' He shook his head. 'You have to leave the chickens alone, Alfie. It's way too dangerous. People get furious when you eat up their chickens. What if someone caught you one night?'

Alfie pulled away the scarf to wipe his muzzle with a paw.

'*Wrow*,' he growled. 'I'm sorry, Tim. I couldn't help it.' He pointed up. 'It's full moon. You know what happens . . .' He tugged at his tail in embarrassment. 'I got the werewolf hunger again. I chose a chicken coop all the way over here on the other side of town, just to be on the safe side. How was I to know that guy would come after me on his motorbike?'

Tim shook his head. 'You know what to do when you get the werewolf hunger. Eat a raw steak from the fridge. A nice juicy one. That helps. Grandpa told you that, remember?'

Alfie nodded. 'There weren't any raw steaks in the fridge, so . . .'

Tim sighed. 'I understand. Of course. Mum forgot to get some new steaks. It's lucky I woke up and saw you were gone. That's why I came looking for you.'

'I'm glad you did,' said Alfie quietly. 'That man had me cornered. I wouldn't have got away if it hadn't been for you.' He laid his head on Tim's shoulder. '*Wrow*, you're my best friend. For now and for ever.'

Tim chuckled. 'Come on, let's get home. We won't tell Mum and Dad. They don't want us running around in the rain at night. If they find out, they won't let us go on the school trip.'

Together they trudged home in the rain.

'And,' Tim asked, 'was it a yummy chicken?'

'It was OK,' Alfie growled. 'I always get feathers between my teeth. It's like biting a pillow.'

Behind them they suddenly heard a familiar drone. Alfie jumped a good metre in the air.

'That's him again!' He dived behind Tim.
'Oh!' said Tim.
'What is it?' growled Alfie.
'Oh, no!'
'What? What?'
'Careful. Here comes . . .'
'What? Tell me. What?'
'An old lady on a chopper.' Tim sniggered.
'What?'

An old lady puttered past on a tiny moped.
She was wearing a big pink helmet and had

an enormous shopping bag on the back of
the moped. Alfie thumped Tim on the
shoulder.

'You pain!'

Tim grinned. 'You fell for it. Come on, let's
go home.'

They raced off down the street.

4

The Flu

Alfie opened his eyes and immediately thought, It's the school trip today. He washed, got dressed and ran downstairs, charged into the kitchen and sat down at the breakfast table with a smile on his face.

'Good morning, Alfie,' said Tim's mother. 'Do you feel like an egg?'

'No, thanks,' Alfie answered. 'I'm not really hungry.'

Tim's mother looked at him thoughtfully, then nodded. 'I understand. It's nerves. You can hardly wait to go on the school trip, but you still need to eat. Otherwise you'll never grow up to be a big werewolf.' Mum laughed and winked at Alfie. 'You can't go off on an empty stomach.'

Alfie gave a deep, happy sigh. He was so lucky to live with Tim and his parents. They knew his secret and loved him anyway.

Each month at full moon, Alfie turned into a wolf at night. Sometimes it happened once a month, sometimes twice, but never more than three times in a row.

Besides Tim and his parents, no one knew Alfie's secret. Alfie didn't remember his own parents. They had abandoned him when they found out he was a werewolf. But Tim's parents had taken him into their house lovingly. They weren't bothered about him being a werewolf. Tim's father even thought it was cool. And Tim was his very best friend, who always protected him. I am so lucky, thought Alfie.

'What are you dreaming about, Alf?'

Tim's father sat down at the table. He had an elephant tea cosy on his head and he was wearing a purple dressing gown that was decorated with little elephants. Bright-red elephants were dangling from his earlobes. Tim's father liked to be different and today he was having an elephant day. He winked at Alfie.

'Er, nothing special,' said Alfie. 'I was thinking about how great it is to live with you. And today Tim and I are going on the school trip together.'

'We think it's great having you here with us too, Alf,' Tim's father said. 'You're a sweet boy and a fabulous werewolf.'

Alfie smiled. 'What's keeping Tim? We have to get going. I've already packed all my stuff.'

'Er, there's a slight problem,' Tim's mother said. She put a boiled egg down in front

of Tim's father and laid a hand on Alfie's shoulder. 'Tim's in bed with the flu. He can't go on the school trip with you.'

Alfie was so shocked he knocked over his teacup.

5

Don't Worry

Alfie jumped up. 'What? Tim, sick? He can't be. He mustn't be. I mean, what about the school trip? I can't go alone, can I? What if I change?' Alfie paced around the table nervously.

'Come on, son, relax,' Mum said, putting Alfie's teacup back on the saucer and wiping the table dry with a cloth. 'It's not a problem. You can stay home too if you like.'

Alfie froze. 'Stay home? And miss the trip?'

Dad shrugged. 'If you don't want to go,

18

we won't make you, but there's nothing to be afraid of.'

He walked over to where the week planner was hanging on the wall. 'Look, you can see here. It won't be full moon again until next week. Tim's marked it with a cross. You'll be long back by then, so you don't need to worry about turning into a werewolf during the school trip.'

Just then the doorbell rang. Alfie walked into the hall.

'You never know,' he mumbled. 'Maybe I'd better stay home anyway.'

He opened the door to a girl with long black hair. Her face was the light-brown colour of coffee with milk.

'Hi, Alfie,' she said. 'You ready?'

Alfie stared at her with big eyes and his glasses slid down to the tip of his nose. 'Noura!'

The girl smiled. She had brown eyes with little specks of gold in them. They were the prettiest eyes Alfie had ever seen.

'You are coming on the school trip, aren't

19

you? Or are you staying here?'

'What are you talking about? Coming on the school trip? Of course I am! I'm all ready. I'll just grab my stuff.'

Alfie did a little skip, grabbed his coat off the hook and ran into the kitchen. 'Um . . . Mum, Dad, I'm off. See you in three days.'

Dad scratched his head under the tea cosy. 'You sure you want to go, Alfie?'

Alfie nodded. 'Sure, it's only two nights. You can get by without me for that long.'

He kissed Tim's father on the forehead and hugged Tim's mother, then he hurried out of the kitchen.

'Wow, he's full of confidence all of a sudden,' Dad said.

Tim's mother smiled. 'Yes . . . Noura. You know what I mean? I think Alfie's a bit crazy about her. He has been ever since he went to her birthday party.'

Dad nodded. 'That's true, I'd forgotten. Clever of Noura to turn him into a daredevil just like that.'

Mum winked at Dad. 'Oh, I remember

you being quite a daredevil too when we'd just met.'

A dreamy look came into Dad's eyes. 'That's true. I was completely fearless, I remember it well. Riding my bike with no hands. Drinking tea without sugar. Crossing the road barefoot. I did it all for you.'

'My hero,' Mum giggled.

Alfie grabbed his backpack and his sleeping bag and walked to the front door. 'Noura, I'm ready.'

'Great, let's go,' Noura said.

'Bye!' Alfie called for the last time, pulling the door shut behind him. In the same instant Tim appeared at the top of the stairs.

'Alfie, wait!' he shouted.

Tim's face was flushed. His forehead was gleaming with sweat and his eyes looked funny.

'Stop him! Don't let him go!'

21

6

Wrong!

Mum stepped into the hall and looked up at Tim, who was holding on to the banister with both hands. His pyjama top was drenched with sweat.

'Young man, what do you think you're doing? Go back to bed this instant.'

'Call Alfie back,' Tim said in a weak voice. 'He can't go on the trip without me.'

Mum shook her head. 'Alfie will be fine. There's nothing to worry about. We checked the week planner. It's not full moon until next week.'

'That's wrong!' Tim shouted, swaying forward dangerously. Mum rushed up the stairs, grabbed him just in time and pushed him back on to the landing. Drops of sweat fell from his forehead as he slumped in Mum's arms.

'Quick, let's get you back into bed,' Mum said. 'You've got quite a temperature and you're delirious.'

Mum pulled Tim back to his room, but he struggled against her with all his might.

'No,' he panted. 'Wait! Listen! I've got a temperature, but I'm not delirious. You know how I always tear the page off the week planner at the end of the week?'

Mum nodded. 'Yes, and you do it very well.'

Tim shook his head. 'Do you know what day it is today?'

Mum smiled. 'Of course. I just checked. It's Monday 12 October.'

Tim sighed. Instead of red he was now deathly pale.

'Wrong,' he whispered. 'Yesterday I

23

forgot to tear off the page because I'd come down with the flu. I didn't give it a second thought.'

'Hold on,' Mum said. 'Hold on now. Which page exactly are you talking about?'

'The page of the week planner. It's a week later than you think. Today is 19 October. There'll be a full moon tonight.'

Mum blinked and stared at Tim silently. A tea cosy in the shape of an elephant came up the stairs. Under it was Tim's father.

'Check your watch!' Mum said.

Dad looked at her with surprise. 'It's half past nine, honey, I can tell you that without looking.'

'Not the time,' Mum said. 'The date! I want to know what day it is!'

Dad smiled. 'I can even tell you that, sweetheart. It's 12 October. We just saw it on the week planner, remember?'

Mum lost her patience. 'Just check your watch! You pig-headed . . . elephant!'

Dad was so startled the tea cosy fell off his head. Quickly he looked at his elephant watch.

'I told you! It's—' For a moment his mouth hung open. '19 October. But that's . . .'

Mum finished the sentence for him, 'A week later than we thought. Couldn't you have checked your watch earlier? Now it's too late!'

She glared at Dad.

'It's full moon tonight. Tonight Alfie will turn into a werewolf. And he thinks it won't happen until next week!'

1
Moving Day

For a moment Tim, Mum and Dad stood deathly still at the top of the stairs, staring at each other. Then Dad ran down the stairs.

'Where are you going?' Mum shouted.

'School. Try to warn Alfie.'

He grabbed the tea cosy, pulled it back down over his head, ran out of the door in his elephant dressing gown, jumped into the car and screeched off down the road. There was a traffic light at the corner. Bad luck! It was red. Gritting his teeth, Dad stamped on the brakes and waited.

Green.

Just then a little old lady started to cross the road. She was very crooked and walked with a stick. Very slowly. On her head she was wearing a pink motorbike helmet.

Nice helmet, thought Dad. Now, if she'd just walk a little bit faster. He beeped the horn as hard as he could. The light turned orange. The old lady stopped where she was, right in front of Dad's car.

Red.

Come on, dear, get moving, thought Dad. The old lady raised her stick.

Green.

She shook it angrily.

Amber.

Red.

Now the old lady started hitting the bonnet of the car. Her mouth kept opening and closing. She didn't have any teeth any more, but it was obvious that she was saying some very nasty things.

Green.

Dad shrunk behind the steering wheel as the minutes crept by.

Amber.

Red.

'Walk on, would you?' Dad said, gnashing his teeth.

Green.

Finally the old lady spat on the windscreen and finished crossing the road.

Amber.

Red.

Dad stamped on the accelerator and tore off. The old lady raised her bony fist.

'Road hog!' she screeched. 'Elephant! No respect for poor old people.' In her rage she kicked over a planter box. 'What you looking at?' she snarled at a passer-by, then went on her way grumbling and growling.

Other pedestrians crossed the road to avoid her.

Dad had already turned the corner.

'I'll still make it,' he mumbled. 'I know a shortcut.'

He shot down a side street called Narrow Lane.

'This will save at least five minutes,' he said to himself, but suddenly there was a gigantic removals van in front of him, almost as wide as the street. Dad stamped on the brakes.

The removals van stopped in front of a house and two big, burly removal men jumped out.

'So,' they said, grinning at Dad, 'let's start with a cuppa.'

They went into the house and Dad took a deep breath. He couldn't possibly get past the removals van. He'd have to back up.

He looked in his rear-view mirror and got the shock of his life. There was another removals van behind him, just as big as the first one. Three removal men climbed out. It must have been moving day on Narrow Lane.

Dad sighed, got out of the car and leant against it. What a nightmare. Caught between two removal vans.

'This is going to take hours,' he groaned. 'I'll never get there in time to warn Alfie now.'

8

A Strange Face

'Ah! I can see Sulphur Forest in the distance already,' Mr French said. 'The farm we'll be staying at for the next two nights is right next to it.'

He was standing at the front of the coach, next to the driver. There were thirty children in the coach. Mr French taught Year 3, Alfie and Noura's class. Sitting next to him was a woman with a rather long nose. That was Miss James, the new Year 4 teacher – Tim's class. She was very happy to be coming on the trip. Not because she was that keen on

31

school trips, but because she was keen on Mr French.

Miss James peered intently through the windscreen. 'So, children, do you see that magnificent forest? A delightful location for a school trip. We can tell horror stories round the campfire and we can experience nature at first hand on our night walk.'

Miss James looked at Mr French out of the corner of her eye and winked. 'That walk in the dark sounds especially cosy,' she giggled. 'Maybe we'll get lost together, Roger.'

Mr French raised an eyebrow. 'I don't think so, Miss James. We have a guide coming to show us around, a hunter who comes here often. He's an expert at finding his way in the dark, so there's very little chance of us getting lost.'

'Fun!' said Noura. 'Will you walk next to me, Alfie? Then I'll feel safe at least.'

Alfie blushed and nodded. For a moment he thought of Tim, at home in bed with a temperature, but that thought disappeared when Noura smiled at him.

'Stupid!' said Rose, a girl with bleached, shoulder-length hair. 'I don't like going for walks in the dark. And I don't like ghost stories either. And my father says campfires are dangerous.'

Mr French sighed. Rose never thought anything was fun. She thought everything was stupid.

'You know what, Rose? If you don't feel like it, why don't you just stay at the farmhouse tonight all by yourself. Then we'll tell stupid ghost stories around a stupid campfire.'

'I'm not doing that,' Rose said. 'I'm not going to spend the night all by myself at a stupid farm.'

Mr French shrugged. 'Then stop whining, Rose.'

Rose glared ahead. 'Stupid!'

The coach bounced down the bumpy dirt road, giving everyone a shaking and making the luggage dance in the racks. Sleeping bags fell down into the aisle.

'I'm really looking forward to that campfire,' Noura said. 'I hope the moon is full. That's so beautiful.'

'Do you like full moons?' asked Alfie, surprised. 'The next one's not till next week.'

'Do you think so?' Noura said. 'I thought it was tonight.'

Alfie looked at her and turned a little red. 'Tonight? But that's not … are you sure?'

Noura shrugged. 'Not really, but we'll see, won't we?' She looked at Alfie with surprise. 'Why do you look so worried all of a sudden? Is something wrong?'

Alfie gave a faint smile. 'Um, no, not at all. I just hope—'

'Yes,' Miss James shouted suddenly. 'Here it is.'

Mr French and Miss James showed the children the dormitories. Mr French was sleeping in the boys' dormitory. Miss James was in with the girls.

They were sleeping in bunk beds. Alfie's

34

bed was next to the window. He rolled his sleeping bag out on the top bunk and looked out of the window. It was too bad Tim couldn't come.

He thought about what Noura had said. She must have made a mistake. There couldn't possibly be a full moon tonight. They'd checked the week planner at home. Tim always put a cross on the days when it was full moon and Tim always looked out for him.

Alfie sat on the top bunk deep in thought for a while longer. He was a bit worried. What if Noura was right? Then he looked up and gasped with fright.

A face was looking in through the window. A pointy face, unshaven, with big ears, cropped hair and fierce eyes.

And those angry eyes were staring straight at him.

9

The Hunter

Alfie was so frightened he tumbled off the bed. Fortunately he was able to grab the steel edge on the way down and hang on with his feet dangling in the air.

'Hey, Alfie, you doing gymnastics or what?' Vincent asked.

Alfie glanced sideways at Vincent, smiled faintly, let go of the side of the bed and landed on the floor.

'I just saw someone.'

'What?'

'There was someone looking in

through the window.'

Vincent walked over to the window, but there was no one in sight. 'Who?'

Alfie shrugged. 'I don't know. A man or maybe a boy. No one I knew anyway.'

'Strange,' Vincent said. 'Maybe we should tell Mr French.'

'Ah, forget it,' said Alfie. 'It was just a nosy parker.'

'A what?'

'A nosy parker. You know what a nosy parker is, don't you?'

'Oh, yeah, sure,' Vincent said. 'You coming? Everybody else is already outside.'

The kids all went into the forest with Mr French leading the way. Miss James stayed behind at the farmhouse to make some soup. Near the farm there was a beautiful clearing.

'An excellent site for a fire,' Mr French said. 'People have made fires here before, you can see that. And we'll make our campfire here tonight. We'll start looking for wood now. There are plenty of sticks and branches lying around.'

'Gathering sticks? What a stupid job,' said Rose. 'What are we going to do with the sticks, sir?'

Mr French gave Rose a weary look.

He bent forward and whispered, 'Try sticking them in your ears, Rose.' Then he strode off.

Alfie and Noura were searching for branches with a group of kids. Vincent, Rudi and Karen were digging a hole.

That was where they were going to put the wood. They had already collected quite a few branches. Alfie was trying extra hard, with Noura watching.

'You OK, Alfie?' Mr French asked.

Alfie nodded, panting and with a bright-red face. 'I'm carrying the heavy branches for Noura,' he said, dragging a long branch into the middle of the clearing.

'Wow, you're really strong, Alfie,' Noura said. 'You sure you don't want me to help?'

Alfie shrugged. 'No, I'm fine, thanks.'

Mr French chuckled. 'This is going to be a fantastic campfire.'

'As long as Rose's ears don't catch fire,' said Alfie.

'What do you mean?' asked Mr French.

'When we light the sticks.'

Mr French thought for a moment, then gave Alfie a look of astonishment. 'You have very sharp hearing, Alfie.'

Alfie smiled.

Suddenly there was a roaring noise. Sand billowed up in the distance. A motorbike was coming towards them, slipping and sliding over the track. The rider's helmet glittered in the sun.

'Ah, here comes our guide,' Mr French said. 'The hunter who will lead us through the forest tomorrow night.'

'What kind of hunter rides a motorbike?' Noura whispered. 'Forests are supposed to be quiet.'

The motorbike stopped next to the pile of firewood and the hunter got off and removed his helmet. Alfie's whole body froze. He felt the blood rush to his face. It was the man who had chased him. The same motorbike, the same hair, the same moustache. The man sniffed and looked at Alfie. Alfie wished the ground could swallow him up. He'd had it now. The hunter would recognize him, and then . . . Oh, no, if only Tim was here.

10
Show-off

The hunter scratched his head, then walked over to Mr French. Alfie let out a sigh. Incredible. The man hadn't recognized him. It didn't make any sense. He'd looked straight at him, hadn't he?

Oh, of course! thought Alfie. The hunter couldn't possibly recognize him. He'd never seen him. He only saw a wolf in his chicken coop.

'What's the matter?' Noura asked quietly. 'Do you know that man? You look like you're scared of him.'

Alfie nodded. 'I scoffed one of his chickens,' he whispered.

'Huh?' said Noura.

'Scared!' Alfie said quickly. 'I scared one of his chickens. For no reason, just for fun, you know.'

Noura giggled softly. 'Scaring chickens? Do you get up to things like that? I never would have thought it.'

The hunter held out his hand. 'Bucket, eh?'

'Er, what do you mean?' said Mr French, surprised.

'That's my name, eh? Sam Bucket. But you can call me Hunter Sam. You're the teacher in charge of the group I'm leading tomorrow night, eh?'

Mr French nodded. 'That's right, eh? I'm Mr French, eh? I mean, um . . . You can call me Mr French.'

The hunter grinned. 'Excellent, Mr French. I hope there aren't any scaredy-cats in your class.'

Mr French raised an eyebrow. 'Why's that, Hunter Sam?'

The hunter smoothed his moustache. 'Well, all kinds of things wander around Sulphur Forest once it's dark, eh?'

'See?' said Rose.

'All kinds of wild animals,' the hunter went on.

'I knew it, I'm staying at the farm,' Rose said.

The hunter looked around and smiled. 'Not so very long ago, for instance, there was a wolf in my henhouse, eh?'

'A wolf?' Mr French said.

'That's right, Mr Teacher, a wolf. And not a little titchy one either. It was a whopper, a big grey one, eh?'

Alfie almost burst out laughing, but quickly clapped his hand over his mouth. What an imagination, he thought. That wolf was small and white.

Smiling, the hunter stroked his moustache. 'I've scared you now, eh?' He looked around and puffed up his chest. 'As long as you're with me, there's nothing to be afraid of. I know Sulphur Forest like my own backyard.

What's more, tomorrow I'll be bringing my friend with me.'

The children looked at him questioningly.

'My gun, eh?' he explained, putting on his helmet and climbing back on to his motorbike. 'Wild animals better stay out of the forest tomorrow night, eh?' Then he roared off.

Mr French watched the motorbike until it disappeared from sight. 'What a windbag,' he mumbled. 'What a show-off with his motorbike and his gun.'

'It's a bit sad having a gun as your best friend,' Noura said. 'I bet he hasn't got any others.'

'See, just what I thought, I knew as much!' Rose shouted. 'A school trip in a forest is dangerous! And now there's wolves here too. I want to go home.'

Vincent, Kevin and a few of the other boys roared with laughter.

'Ha-ha, Rose would rather go to a petting zoo,' Vincent screamed. 'She'd be safe there.'

'You don't need to act so brave,' Noura said. 'What would you do if you ran into a wolf?'

'Ha, I'd kick it,' Vincent said. 'They're dirty, sneaky, horrible animals. Watch out, Rose. There's a wolf in the forest and it's going to eat you up.'

The other children started laughing. Alfie didn't join in. He didn't think the joke was funny. Mr French clapped his hands angrily.

'That's enough! There's no need to tease Rose. And Rose, there's nothing to be scared of. There are no wolves here!'

Just then a fearful cry sounded from the farm. Everyone turned in fright.

'Miss James!' Mr French said. 'Quick, to the farm.'

11

Soup Thief

Miss James was standing in the doorway, looking pale and holding a large soup ladle. Mr French hurried up to her.

'Miss James, what's going on here? We heard your scream from the forest.'

Miss James had a wild expression on her face.

'My soup! He ran off with my soup. He licked out the pan.'

Mr French looked at Miss James with astonishment.

'Who? What are you talking about?

Who licked out the pan?'

'That boy! The, the . . .' Miss James didn't know what to say, that was how furious she was. White froth spattered from her lips.

'Which boy?' Mr French asked. 'Who was it?'

'A . . . a scruffy lout! I walked into the kitchen and there he was with his head in the saucepan. He was shocked to hear me and he looked up. A pointy face, big ears, soup all over his chin. The saucepan fell over. Half the soup ended up on the floor. He'd already slobbered up the rest.' She waved the ladle over her head. 'If I get hold of him, I'll show him. I'll box those big ears of his!'

Suddenly she gave Mr French a look of total misery and spread her arms wide. 'I've had such a fright, Roger. I need a hug.'

Mr French took a step backwards. 'Er, er, let's think for a moment, Miss James. Who do you think it was?'

'How would I know?' Miss James wailed.

Mr French quickly moved over behind Alfie and Noura.

'Maybe a tramp,' Noura said. 'Someone who hasn't had a thing to eat for days. Someone who's alone and miserable and starving.'

'Alone and miserable?' whispered Miss James. 'What about me? I can't even get a hug.'

But nobody was listening to her. Vincent started laughing and nudged Rudi and Ahmed.

'There goes Noura again,' he jeered. 'We're supposed to feel sorry for the soup thief.'

Alfie scratched his head. 'I think I saw him, sir.'

'Who? The soup thief?'

Alfie nodded. 'When I was sitting on my bed in the dormitory, he peeped in through the window.'

'Oh, the nosy parker?' said Vincent, who had stopped laughing.

'Yeah, him,' Alfie said.

A few of the children gasped in fright.

'See,' said Rose. 'I knew it! As if things weren't bad enough already. Now we've got a soup-stealing peeper! I think we should go home right away. This school trip is going to be one big disaster. All the signs are pointing that way. No one wants to wake up tomorrow in a blood-soaked bed.' Rose stopped talking and looked around with a serious expression. 'If they wake up at all!'

The other children gaped at her.

'Come off it,' Mr French blurted, 'a hungry tramp licks out our soup pot. It's annoying. But you don't need to turn it into a story full of mayhem and murder! We'll save those stories for around the campfire,' he added quietly.

Miss James clapped her hands. She wasn't feeling miserable any more. 'That's right, boys and girls. We're here to have a fun, sociable school trip. And we're not going to let a soup thief ruin it for us. He ran off and he's not going to bother us any more. We'll just forget all about him. I've made a stack of sandwiches. Is anyone hungry?'

All of the kids gave big nods.

'Inside then.'

The children followed Miss James into the farmhouse. Alfie paused on the doorstep, looking back at the forest for a moment.

'Is something wrong?' Noura asked.

Alfie shrugged. 'I don't know. I just thought . . .' He shook his head. 'No, nothing. Forget it.'

'Hey, are you coming or not?' Mr French called. 'You must be famished after all that work. We'll eat now and then we're going to build a fabulous campfire.'

Alfie and Noura hurried into the farmhouse.

Outside, the undergrowth moved. For a moment the branches parted. Two gleaming eyes peered out from between the leaves. A soft panting noise could be heard.

12

The Campfire

'OK, guys. Throw some more branches on,'
Mr French said, walking around the campfire
and nodding approvingly. Everything was as
it should be: the children's stomachs were
full, the beds had been made and nobody
was thinking about the soup thief any
more. The children were sitting around the
campfire, which was burning nicely. They
had buckets of water ready for emergencies.
The flames were leaping up and crackling
sparks were shooting up into the sky.

'Campfires are nice and warm, aren't they?'

Noura whispered. 'And cosy too. Don't you think?'

Alfie nodded and looked up at the sky. It was cloudy. The sun had set and it was slowly growing darker. There wasn't a star to be seen. The children were sitting on logs they had dragged up themselves. The red glow shone on their faces. Miss James handed out cups of hot cocoa, then sat down too. Mr French brought out a big fat book to read.

'Time for a nice horror story!'

Miss James cooed. 'Ooh, exciting! Will you come and sit next to me, Roger?'

Mr French acted like he hadn't heard her. 'This book is called *The Horror Bus*. It's full of scary stories.' He grinned and looked at the children's faces with his eyes shining red from the fire.

'Time for a story about . . .' He held the book in front of his face and peered over the top of it. 'A werewolf!'

Alfie held his breath. Noura moved a bit closer. Alfie felt her trembling. 'What is it?' he whispered.

'Werewolves are really scary,' Noura said quietly. 'I saw a film about a werewolf once. Afterwards I couldn't sleep for three nights.'

Alfie swallowed audibly. 'Um, maybe only some werewolves are scary. Maybe there are friendly werewolves too. Don't you think?'

Noura burst out laughing. 'Friendly werewolves? That's a bit like friendly sharks. They bite your leg off with a smile on their face.'

Alfie chuckled but looked upset.

'Alfie, Noura, are you paying attention?'

Then Mr French started to read and everyone was as quiet as a mouse. The story was about a werewolf that lived in a tower block. Two boys, Peter and Barry, went looking for the werewolf.

Mr French was good at reading out loud. Sometimes he kept his voice quiet, sometimes he cranked up the volume. Noura listened without even blinking and slid closer and closer to Alfie. The story got more and more exciting. Mr French stood up and walked around the circle while he read:

'Patience,' panted Peter. 'It could happen any minute now, because the full moon has broken through the clouds.

It is the hour of the werewolf.'

Their teacher's voice was a whisper and in the glow of the flames his face looked ghostly. For a moment he was silent, staring at their faces. It was deathly quiet. The children waited tensely.

Even Rose had forgotten that she thought campfires and horror stories were stupid.

Alfie looked up. The sky was still covered with clouds. There were no stars and no moon in sight. Mr French read on. Alfie looked sideways at Noura, who had her hands over her mouth.

'Luckily it's not a full moon,' Alfie whispered. 'There's nothing to be afraid of.'

In the same instant the clouds parted, just like that. They drifted apart, revealing hundreds of stars and the moon – a beautiful full moon.

'Pay attention,' Mr French said. 'Now it gets really exciting.'

13

It Starts with an Itch

Alfie had stopped listening to Mr French's voice. He was staring at the moon. The full moon. How could that be? Had Tim made a mistake? Or was there something wrong with the week planner? Alfie looked around cautiously. The children were listening tensely to Mr French. Noura was sitting very close to him. She was listening to the story with her mouth open and seemed to find it very exciting.

Alfie looked back up at the moon. Maybe nothing will happen, he thought. Maybe I

won't change tonight. He scratched his hand. It was itchy. He knew that feeling. It was no ordinary itch, it was a werewolf itch. He looked down and was so shocked he almost screamed. His hand was already covered with hair. White hair.

Quickly he stuck his hand between his legs. But his other hand started to itch straightaway as well. Suddenly it too was covered with hair. His fingernails gleamed in the moonlight. They were long and getting longer, slowly changing into claws. He looked around in a panic. What now? He was in the middle of changing, but no one had noticed anything yet. All eyes were on

Mr French. He was an extremely exciting reader. That was lucky, because Alfie could feel his ears gradually stretching. His face was itchy too. He felt it on his cheeks. His whole body began to itch. No amount of scratching could stop the werewolf itch. He felt his tail growing out of him.

I have to get away from here! Alfie thought. I have to hide before someone sees me. Just then Noura grabbed his arm and squeezed it, but she didn't look at him. All her attention was on Mr French.

One of the boys in the story had just discovered that the other boy was the werewolf. A sigh passed through the children.

'No!' whispered Rose.

Carefully Alfie slipped his arm out of Noura's grip.

'Exciting, isn't it?' whispered Noura.

Alfie tried to say something, but the only noise that came up out of his throat was a soft growl. *'Wrow.'*

He covered his mouth with his paws and

immediately realized that his nose had changed into a muzzle. Noura still hadn't noticed. Alfie knew *one* thing. He had to get out of there as fast as he could. Very cautiously he slid backwards. The campfire crackled and sparks fanned up in the night sky. Towards the full moon.

Mr French was using lots of gestures to explain how horrific the werewolf in the story was. Alfie slid back out of the circle. Now he was looking at the other children's backs. He felt the bushes behind him.

'And then Peter sees the werewolf,' Mr French read. A soft gasp of horror passed through the circle.

'Stupid!' muttered Rose. 'Why doesn't he run away?'

Now! thought Alfie, rolling backwards and disappearing into the undergrowth.

14

A Howling Wolf

Alfie crawled out on the other side of the bushes. In the silence of the woods he could clearly hear Mr French's voice and through the leaves he could see the children sitting in a circle.

He saw Noura too. Suddenly he felt very alone. Why could the others snuggle around the campfire together and not me? he thought.

'Because at the moment you're a werewolf, you twerp,' said a voice inside his head. 'They'd probably be scared to death if they saw you. That wouldn't be much fun, would it?'

Suddenly Alfie thought of the first time he had changed into a werewolf. It had happened the night he turned seven. He almost scared himself to death when he saw his reflection in the window. Fortunately he'd met his grandfather. Grandpa was a werewolf too. He'd been a werewolf his whole life and Grandpa was more than happy with that.

'You get used to it,' he'd told Alfie.

And it was true. Alfie was gradually getting used to it.

But now I really would rather be sitting in front of the campfire, he thought.

'Stop dawdling and get going!' the voice said. 'Imagine Noura seeing you like this, with all that hair and those teeth. What do you think would happen then?'

I've got to get away from here! thought Alfie. Before they discover that I'm gone and start looking for me. If only Tim was here!

He growled softly, turned around and shot off under the dark trees. He didn't know where he was going. He just ran. High above the treetops the full moon floated along behind him.

His shoes pinched and he could hardly breathe in his clothes. His shirt was starting to tear. Quickly he pulled off his shoes and his coat, but he still felt like he was suffocating, so he took off the rest of his clothes. It was an enormous relief. Finally Alfie felt free. Only his glasses were still on his nose.

He dropped so that he was standing on all fours and looked up at the moon. His mouth opened. All by itself, a long extended howl came up out of his throat. Alfie the Werewolf howled at the full moon.

At the campfire Mr French looked up in fright. He'd just finished the story. He sat down next to Miss James and clapped the book shut.

'What was that noise?' asked Miss James, moving closer to Mr French.

'I . . . I don't know.'

Mr French looked around and saw the children's frightened faces.

'It was a wolf,' Rose shouted. 'See, I told you so. It's all going to go wrong, of course. You'll see. That Mr Bucket warned us about wolves. Soon we'll be surrounded by a whole club of them.'

'Nonsense!' Mr French said. 'There is no such thing as a club for wolves. And Mr Bucket was just telling stories. He was trying to wind you up. That was a stray dog, that's all.'

He started to laugh. 'My horror story has made quite an impression on you. I bet that you were frightened half to death. You're probably all thinking that was a werewolf you just heard. But of course, we all know that werewolves don't exist. Don't we?'

There were a few sniggers. The boys nudged each other. Of course. Everyone knew that werewolves were made up.

Astonished, Noura looked at the empty spot next to her. Where was Alfie?

Just then another terrifying howl filled the air. Mr French jumped.

'Miss James, I think it's time we got back

to the farm. It's already late and the fire is almost out.'

'Call me Jenny, silly,' Miss James whispered. She moved to lean against him, but Mr French stepped away at the same time and she fell over. Slightly embarrassed, she scrambled back up and brushed the sand off her clothes. Mr French didn't seem to have noticed a thing. He started giving instructions.

'Vincent, Rahid, Larissa, your turn. You know where the buckets are.'

They jumped up and used the buckets of water to douse the smouldering remains of the campfire. Mr French clapped his hands.

'Come on, kids, don't dawdle, please. It's been a long day. You have to get to bed.'

As they left, he looked over his shoulder at the forest. Behind him he heard the sound of snapping twigs. As if something was shuffling through the undergrowth. He looked ahead quickly. A horror story like that even gives *me* scary thoughts, he reflected.

Just to be on the safe side he went to walk next to Miss James. She smiled at him.

'So, Roger,' she whispered. 'We're having a cosy walk together after all, aren't we?'

Mr French burst into a coughing fit and quickly strode ahead. Noura wondered again where Alfie was. She couldn't see him anywhere. Maybe he'd gone back early to go to the toilet or something, she thought.

Alfie was running through the forest and feeling as free as a real wild wolf. He did a cheerful pee on a big tree. Then he ran on.

Suddenly he remembered his classmates and Noura. I mustn't go too far, he thought. I have to be back in my bed before morning. He stopped with a jerk. What if Mr French checks the beds? He had to go back. Right this minute. He had to try to sneak into bed unseen and then hide under the blankets. Tomorrow morning I'll just be Alfie again, he thought. That won't be a problem. He had to go back.

Which way was it again? He stuck his

nose up in the air and sniffed. He could smell the extinguished campfire very clearly. He just had to follow that smell. Easy peasy.

Suddenly it was as if a storm had struck. There was something in the undergrowth. Bushes swished back and forth, branches snapped, shadows moved. Two pointy grey ears appeared. A broad grey wolf's head popped up from the bushes right in front of Alfie's eyes.

'Alfie!' the big wolf growled. At least, that was what it *seemed* to growl.

15

Surprise Visitor

Alfie saw a big wolf stepping out of the bushes and was frozen to the spot with fright. Who is this wolf? he thought. And how does it know my name?

Then he saw something else that was strange. The big wolf was wearing a dressing gown with little wolves all over it. The wolf raised one of its paws. Alfie stared at it and saw that it wasn't a paw at all. It was a grey woollen glove.

And there were grey wolf slippers on the wolf's feet.

'Alfie,' the wolf said again in a slightly muffled voice. Then it grabbed its own ears and pulled the head off its body. Alfie's mouth dropped open and his tongue rolled out.

'Dad!' he growled.

Standing in front of him was Tim's father. He was holding a wolf mask in his hands, a wolf mask that looked just like the real thing. He was sweaty, with a red face and wet hair.

'Phew, it's really stuffy under one of those heads. I don't know how you stand it.'

Alfie could still hardly believe his eyes. '*Wrow*, Dad! What are you doing here?'

Tim's father wiped the sweat off his brow. 'Well, Alfie, it's like this. I'm here to warn you.'

'To warn me? *Wrow*, what about, Dad?'

Dad pointed up at the moon. 'Tim forgot to tear the page off the week planner. I'm here to warn you that there's a full moon tonight. And that you'll turn into a werewolf this evening.'

'OK,' Alfie growled.

Dad looked at him for a moment without speaking. 'But, um, you've already figured that out, of course.'

Alfie looked Dad over once more from head to toe, from his sweaty face to his wolf slippers. 'Why are you dressed up all silly like that?'

'Silly?'

'Well, with the slippers and the wolf mask and that.'

Dad nodded. 'Oh, that. Well, you see, I didn't want to be too conspicuous in this forest. That's why I couldn't come dressed as an elephant. Because there aren't any elephants around here. So I thought, why not a wolf? And then I drove straight to the fancy-dress shop. As a wolf I could come to warn you without attracting any attention. I didn't want the other kids to see me. I thought, maybe they'd think you were a wimp, that you can't get by without us. That's why I came in disguise, see?'

Alfie gazed at Dad. It was clear that he meant every word. Alfie felt a lump in his throat. Tim's parents were sweet and it was very obvious that they loved him. They did crazy things like this for him.

'Thanks,' he growled.

Tim's father grinned. 'Besides, I love dressing up anyway. You know that. I love being different.' He looked at Alfie for a moment. 'So, what do you think? Do you want to come home with me? You can. I'll phone and say you were taken ill all of a sudden.'

Alfie thought about it for a long time. If he went home now, his problems would be solved. No one would discover his secret and he'd be safe. But what would Noura think? He shook his head.

'I'm not coming, Dad. I can't keep running away my whole life. I am who I am. I'll manage.'

'You sure?' Tim's father asked.

'*Wrow*, definitely! Tomorrow evening we're going for a nice walk in the woods. With a hunter as a guide. He knows his way around here really well.'

'A hunter? But what if you turn into a werewolf again?'

Alfie shrugged. 'Then, um, I'll hide. But maybe it won't happen. Maybe the moon won't come out. Then I won't feel any moonlight and I might not change.'

Dad laid a hand on Alfie's shoulder. 'You sure, son?'

Alfie hesitated for a moment, then gave a very firm nod.

'Well, I guess you'll be all right then.' Dad scratched Alfie on the head, between his ears. 'I'm proud of you, Alfie. But Mum and Tim are very anxious to hear how you're doing, so I'll hurry off home now.' He wrapped his arms around Alfie and gave him a hug. They stood there for a moment looking at each other without Dad showing any sign of wanting to leave.

'Um, Dad, I have to hurry back to the farm,' Alfie growled.

'Oh, of course, son. I'll go back to the car then.' Dad pointed to a spot somewhere on the other side of the bushes. 'It's over there on the edge of the forest somewhere. A fair way away from your farm. No one saw me. So I'll leave again unseen now. You'll be careful?'

Alfie nodded.

'I'm off then,' said Dad, but he still showed no sign of moving.

'*Wrow*, go on, Dad. You really don't need to worry. I'll manage.'

'OK, I'm off then. Bye, son. See you soon. The day after tomorrow.'

Finally Dad shuffled away from Alfie, pulling the wolf mask back down over his head. 'You sure you don't want to come with me?'

Alfie held up one paw and waved. 'Bye, Dad.'

Tim's father nodded, shrugged and disappeared between the bushes. Now and then Alfie saw his ears poking up over the leaves. Then he was gone. Alfie was alone again under the full moon.

Straight back to the farm, he thought. I hope they haven't noticed I'm missing.

He dropped forward and ran to the farm on all fours. Once he got there he hid behind a tree. There were no lights on in the dormitories, he could see that much. Everyone had probably gone to bed by now. But the light was still on in one room. That was where Mr French and Miss James were, of course. Alfie crept over to that one room and pressed himself up against the wall under the window ledge. The window was slightly open and the teachers' voices drifted out.

'Another glass of wine, Roger?' Miss James said. 'It'll put a smile on your face.'

'No, thank you, Miss James. I'll just go and check on the boys. Make sure they're all asleep. Then I'm going to bed too. I'm exhausted.'

'Call me Jenny. Can't we relax a little without the children?'

Alfie almost burst out laughing and covered his mouth with his paw. Miss James wouldn't take no for an answer.

'Miss James, we're here to look after the children. I hope you understand that.'

A chair slid back loudly.

'I'll go and check on the girls in a minute,' Miss James said. 'First I'll grab a breath of fresh air. I just love the smell of the forest.'

Oops, she's coming outside. What now? thought Alfie. How can I get inside without her seeing me?

Suddenly the window slid up further. Miss James stuck her head out. She looked from left to right and took a deep breath. Alfie didn't dare move.

16

Rose

Making as little noise as possible, Alfie looked up. Miss James's nose was sticking out over the window ledge. It wasn't a pleasant sight. Alfie could see the hairs in her nostrils. He watched the way her nose moved when she sucked in the air.

'Lovely,' she said. 'Nice and healthy forest air.'

Miss James's hands appeared over the edge of the window ledge as she bent out even more. If she looked down now she would see him, get the fright of her life and start

75

screaming. And then everyone would come out to have a look. And then . . . Alfie couldn't think any further than that. His heart was in his mouth.

'What a lovely night, Roger. Don't you think it's terribly romantic with the full moon shining in?'

'If you ask me, you've breathed in more than enough of that forest air,' Mr French said. 'If you don't watch out your nose will fall off. You really have to go and check the girls now. I'll lock the outside door. Then I'll go and look in on the boys.'

Miss James sighed deeply, then breathed in one last dose of forest air. 'Bah,' she said. 'You don't have a romantic bone in your body.'

Her head disappeared inside and the window banged shut. Alfie growled with relief. He was trembling. The outside door, he thought. I have to get inside before Mr French locks it.

He ran straight to the door and pushed the handle down with one paw. Fortunately it wasn't locked yet and he was able to slip inside cautiously.

The hall was full of dark shadows from the planter boxes with palms that lined the walls. Now I have to make it to the dormitory, thought Alfie. And then into bed, without anyone seeing me.

Alfie crept down the hall on his wolf toes, sneaking from planter box to planter box. He was already halfway when the door at the end of the hall opened.

'Goodnight, Jenny,' Mr French said.

Alfie froze for a moment, like a cartoon character. He looked left, right. On his right there was a door with a little man on it. Alfie pushed it open, shot in and closed it behind him. With his back against the door he stayed there in the darkness listening.

He heard Mr French's footsteps in the hall. The teacher was walking in his socks and they were very soft footsteps that an ordinary boy wouldn't have heard, but Alfie had super-sensitive werewolf hearing. Mr French's footsteps came up to the door, then carried on. Thank goodness, his teacher hadn't seen him.

He's at the back door, thought Alfie. Now I can slip into the boys' dormitory.

Just then the door opened. A hand flicked the light switch and in a flash the room was brightly lit. A girl was standing in the doorway. It was Rose.

17

A Wolf, Ha-ha

Rose was standing dead still in the doorway. She had accidentally chosen the wrong toilets, that was obvious. She'd gone into the hall in the dark and hadn't paid attention to the symbol on the door. This wasn't the girls' toilets. She looked at the creature standing before her. It definitely wasn't a girl.

But it wasn't a boy either. It was a wolf. A white wolf, standing upright, like a person. The strange thing was that this wolf was wearing glasses. A wolf, ha-ha. Impossible. Wolves don't hang around toilets wearing glasses.

Rose almost burst out laughing. She almost screamed with laughter. Rose actually wanted to yell. She could see the way the wolf was looking at her. She saw its sharp claws. She saw its shining teeth. It was too horrible to be true. The room began to spin.

'Ha-ha,' said Rose in a feeble voice. Then her legs swished out from under her as the walls and ceiling spun away. Everything went dark, as if someone had turned off the light.

Alfie stood motionless, still frozen to the spot. He looked at Rose, who was lying still on the floor. She'd fainted.

Bad luck for her, good luck for me, thought Alfie. I thought I was a goner.

Quickly he turned off the light, stepped over Rose and peeked around the corner. Mr French was still at the outside door. The lock was being difficult. Alfie heard him mumble while he struggled with the key.

They could oil this lock now and then.

You stupid, stubborn thing, give me a break, why don't you?'

Mr French kicked the door.

'Ow!' he shouted, dancing around on one foot.

Lucky again, thought Alfie, turning and creeping off to the boys' dormitory, where the door was ajar. Alfie listened in the doorway and heard a loud uneven rustling. The breathing of some twenty boys. Soft snoring was coming from a couple of them.

Alfie stuck his head into the dormitory. The moon was shining in through the thin curtains and by the looks of things all of the

other boys were asleep. Alfie pattered past the beds on all fours, gliding like a shadow to his own bunk above Vincent.

He had almost reached his bed. Vincent was sleeping peacefully. Alfie looked back. Mr French would come in any minute now to check that everybody was asleep. He stood up.

All he had to do now was climb up on to his bed – carefully, making sure he didn't wake up Vincent – then slip into the sleeping bag before Mr French came in. Suddenly a hand grabbed him by the back of the neck.

'No, not that!' a voice said.

18

Loud Snoring

Alfie froze. For a few seconds he looked like a stuffed wolf, as motionless as the shadows on the floor. His eyes wide open. His hair standing on end. He felt the hand on the back of his neck.

Uh-oh! thought Alfie.

'Not that,' the voice said again. 'Mum, please, I hate spinach.'

Huh? thought Alfie.

'Come on, Mum, I want a Coke.'

Slowly, Alfie turned his head. The hand stayed where it was on the back of his neck.

It was Sven's hand. Sven was in the top bunk next to Alfie's and he was lying on his back with his eyes closed. His arm was hanging out of the bed and his hand was draped limply over Alfie's neck.

'I want a Coke, Mum,' Sven said. 'And a Big Mac too, please.'

Alfie growled softly. Idiot! It was nothing at all. Sven's hand had flopped on to his neck by accident. He wasn't even awake. He was dreaming about his mother. He didn't know a thing.

Carefully, Alfie moved Sven's hand away from his neck.

'No, Mum, don't, don't do it,' Sven groaned, pulling his hand back into his sleeping bag, but he didn't wake up.

The dormitory door swung open. Alfie heard Mr French's socks sliding over the floor and acted instantly.

With one leap he was up on the top bunk. No time to pull on his pyjamas. He zipped open the sleeping bag, slipped into it, pulled it up over his ears and lay there listening.

84

Mr French walked past the beds, straightening blankets here and there, making sure no one could fall out of one of the top bunks and listening to see whether everyone was really asleep. Alfie heard Mr French approaching and crept further down into his sleeping bag.

Mr French checked Vincent first. He was sleeping calmly. Then he saw that Alfie was hidden away at the bottom of his sleeping bag. Mr French frowned. 'That boy will suffocate down there,' he whispered to himself. 'I'd better open that sleeping bag a little.' Very carefully he took hold of the top of Alfie's sleeping bag.

Alfie broke into a cold sweat.

'Alfie, come up out of the sleeping bag a little,' his teacher whispered.

All Alfie could do was growl. '*Wrow!*'

Startled, Mr French dropped the sleeping bag. Had he heard properly? Alfie must be having a very strange dream. Mr French hesitated. Maybe I should just let him sleep, he thought. But what a strange noise that was.

Just then Sven started thrashing from side to side. 'No, Mum, no cabbage either!'

Mr French turned around quickly to Sven. 'Shhh,' he whispered. 'You'll wake everyone up.' He patted Sven on the shoulder. 'You don't have to eat any cabbage here. Go back to sleep now.'

A smile appeared on Sven's face. He turned on to his side. 'Thanks, Mum,' he said.

'You're welcome,' whispered Mr French.

He looked over at Alfie one last time. Loud, rhythmic snoring was rising up out of the sleeping bag. It sounded rather strange for a boy, more like a grizzly bear really. The teacher yawned. Oh well, forget it, he thought. Alfie is probably a very deep sleeper. Some people just happen to snore louder than others. I'm going to hit the sack too.

He turned and walked over to his own bed, close to the door. Alfie heard the teacher moving away. Phew, the snoring noises had helped. Now he was out of danger. He could relax and go to sleep.

Tomorrow morning he would just be a

boy called Alfie Span again. He growled and rolled on to his back. Just before falling asleep he thought of something. His clothes were still out there in the forest. He had forgotten to bring them back with him. Oh well, luckily he had a tracksuit and trainers with him. Alfie yawned. Tomorrow, he thought. Now I'm going to sleep.

He stared out over the edge of his sleeping bag at the full moon. His eyes were almost closed. A figure was standing outside the window and peering in through the glass

with yellow eyes. The figure was panting. Its tongue hung out of his mouth and its hairy ears stuck straight up. After a while it turned away and there was no one left at the window.

I'm already dreaming, thought Alfie, turning over on to his side.

19

A Hunter?!

Tim's father woke with a yawn, 'Uwaaah!'
Mum turned over and screamed.

A pair of yellow eyes in a shaggy, hairy head were staring at her from the pillow next to hers.

'Goodness! Is that thing lying there between us again? Will you please stop leaving that wolf's head on your pillow at night? You scared the living daylights out of me.'

'Do I really have to stop?' asked Dad, sitting up straight and lifting the wolf mask up with both hands. 'I want to keep it close by. I'm trying to imagine what it's like to be a wolf. Then I'll understand how Alfie feels at full moon.'

'That's very sweet of you,' Mum said. 'But I'd rather you didn't bring it to bed with you.'

Dad swung his legs over the edge of the bed and turned the wolf mask around to look at it from the other side. 'You know, something's bothering me, but I'm not sure what.'

Mum sat down next to him on the side of the bed. 'Is it something to do with Alfie? You said he was doing well.'

Dad nodded. 'I thought he was, but it was something he said.'

'What did he say?'

Dad rubbed his temples. 'I'm trying to remember. Everything was fine. He said that he'd manage. Tonight they're going for a walk in the forest. A hunter is going to show them around.'

For a moment it was dead quiet in the

bedroom. Sunlight shone in through the curtains. Mum tried to catch her breath.

'A hunter?' She jumped up, grabbed Dad by the shoulders and started shaking him. 'Did I hear that correctly? Did you say *a hunter?*'

'Y-y-yes,' said Dad.

'Our Alfie is going into the forest with a hunter?' Mum shouted. 'When it's full moon again tonight? Do you know what hunters do when they see wolves?'

Dad tried to answer but she was shaking him too hard.

'They shoot them!' Mum shouted. 'Hunters have guns. Hunters love guns. And when they get a chance, they start shooting.'

'Sh-shooting? But not when the other kids are there? Surely not?'

Finally Mum let go of Dad's shoulders. His head was spinning and he toppled sideways on to the bed.

'Shooting,' Mum said. She had turned as white as a sheet. Suddenly the bedroom door opened and Tim came into the room.

'What's going on?' he said. 'What's all the shouting about?'

'Alfie is going into the forest tonight with a hunter,' Mum said. Tim's eyes grew larger.

'Alone?'

'No, with the other kids,' Dad said. 'But he might turn into a wolf again. And if he does, the hunter might see him and what then?'

Tim stared at his parents for a few seconds. 'Why don't we just go and get him?'

'Because he doesn't want us to,' Dad explained. 'Alfie doesn't want to keep running away. He wants to join in with the other kids. And he's actually right. But this is dangerous.'

Tim spun around and ran up to his room. Less than a minute later he was back, fully dressed.

'What are you doing?' Mum asked.

'Someone has to keep an eye on Alfie,' Tim said. 'And there's really only one person who can do a good job of it.'

'Who?' Dad asked.

Tim tied the laces of his trainers and

looked up. 'Grandpa Werewolf. He knows his way around forests. He can watch out for Alfie without anyone seeing him.'

Mum got some colour back in her face. 'Maybe you're right, Tim, but where can we find Grandpa Werewolf?'

'In the park?' Tim suggested. 'That's where Alfie first met him. I'll find him, even if I have to spend all day searching.'

Tim ran downstairs.

'Wait!' Mum shouted. 'You can't go outside. You're ill, remember?'

Tim was already at the front door. 'Don't worry,' he called back. 'I'm as good as better. My temperature has almost gone.'

'Tim!' Dad shouted, but the front door had already slammed shut.

20

Punishment

'It's true,' Rose said. 'I saw it with my own eyes.'

Vincent tried to keep a straight face. 'Tell us again, Rose. I didn't hear you properly. What did you see?'

'A wolf!' Rose screamed. 'Last night in the boys' toilets.'

It was dead quiet for a moment at the breakfast table. All faces turned to Rose. No one was blinking. Mouths were agape. Then everyone burst out laughing. Only Noura didn't laugh.

'I think you're all being mean,' she said. 'There's no need to laugh at Rose.'

Alfie came into the breakfast room in his tracksuit. Astonished, he took in all the smiling faces. 'What's up?' he asked.

'Rose went into the wrong toilets by accident,' Dave shouted.

'And she got such a fright . . .' Vincent went on, hiccuping with laughter, 'that she saw a wolf.'

'Go on, laugh,' Rose shouted. 'It was a wolf. I know what I saw. It had glasses.'

'Water glasses,' screeched Vincent, 'or wine glasses? Or did it have glasses just like Alfie's?' He laughed so hard he almost fell off his chair. 'Did you go to the toilet last night, Alfie?'

Alfie blushed. 'Um, yes.'

'Then it's obvious,' Vincent sniggered.

'Rose went into the boys' toilets by accident and saw Alfie. She got such a fright she thought he was a wolf.'

Once again everyone burst out laughing. Noura gave Alfie a look that was full of sympathy. Rose stamped her foot angrily.

'Laugh away, stupid. It wasn't Alfie. It was a wolf. I'm not mad, you know.'

Just then the doors to the kitchen swung open. Mr French and Miss James came in carrying trays of bread rolls.

'I'm glad to see you so happy,' Mr French said. 'You're laughing so hard we could hear you in the kitchen.' He started to hand out the rolls.

'I want to go home,' said Rose. 'I don't want to stay here another minute.'

Mr French looked at Rose with surprise. 'What is it this time, Rose?'

'There was a wolf in the toilets.'

Mr French put the tray down on the table and took a very deep breath. 'I've had enough, Rose. You keep trying to ruin this school trip. You come up with one weird story after another, but this takes the cake!'

'But I—'

'Be quiet! I don't want to hear another word out of you. Go to the dormitory and stay there all day. We'll decide later whether you're allowed on the forest walk.'

'But, sir, I really did see—'

'Silence!'

Mr French looked like he might explode. He pointed to the door. Rose didn't say another word. She got up silently and shuffled out of the room.

This is terrible, thought Alfie. Rose is getting punished, and it's all my fault. He ate his bread roll in silence.

21

Sneaking

After breakfast they were allowed outside to play. Later they were going to visit a windmill.

Alfie already knew what he had to do: he had to sneak into the forest to look for his clothes. If only Tim had been there. He would have helped him, but now he had to do it alone. At least he knew more or less where they were.

In his pocket he had a folded plastic bag to put his clothes in. Now all he had to do was slip away without anyone noticing.

Some of the boys were playing football. Others were climbing trees or just running around. The girls were still in their dorm. Noura was probably comforting Rose.

Noura was so sweet, she was always helpful and kind to everyone. A really nice girl, thought Alfie, but I mustn't let her find out that I'm a werewolf. That would be a disaster, because she thinks werewolves are horrific.

He looked around and saw that no one was paying him any attention. Quickly he shot off into the bushes.

Noura came out of the door just in time to see someone disappearing into the bushes. Hey, she thought, that looks like Alfie. Where's he going?

The other girls came out too. Except for Rose, of course; she was being punished and sitting inside sulking.

'Noura, you playing?' called Natasha.

'What?'

'Football with the boys.'

Noura thought for a moment. There was

still no sign of Alfie. Then she shook her head. 'No, I don't feel like it.'

'OK,' Natasha shouted.

Screaming and yelling, the girls stormed over to the boys and tried to steal the ball off them. Mr French and Miss James joined in too. Miss James wasn't very good at it. Quite often, when she went for the ball, she kicked Mr French instead.

'Ow!' roared Mr French, after she got him on the shin for the third time. 'Can't you be a bit careful? Or are you doing it on purpose?'

Miss James smiled. 'Not at all. What makes you say that?'

Noura stood there watching for a while. I wonder where Alfie's got to, she thought. He acts a bit strange sometimes. It's as if he's got something to hide. But what? And why would he go into the forest all by himself? What if he got lost?

Noura thought for a moment, then made up her mind. I'll go and look for him, she decided. She glanced back at the others as the ball whizzed through the air. Miss James kicked Mr French in the calf muscle. 'Oh, sorry, Roger. I really was going for the ball.'

Mr French grabbed his leg. 'The ball is over there, near Diane!' he shouted. 'Are you blind or what?' He limped off angrily. Miss James didn't say a word and smiled to herself.

'Maybe you're the one who's blind, Roger,' she whispered.

Seeing that no one was looking in her direction, Noura quickly slipped into the bushes and walked into the forest to look for Alfie. Mr French saw Noura leaving and scratched his head. 'Um, I'm not playing any more,' he called.

'Oh, Roger, don't be such a spoilsport,' Miss James said. 'It won't be half as much fun without you.'

The ball rolled towards her. Miss James took aim and gave the ball an almighty wallop.

'Goal!' screamed Vincent.

For a moment Mr French gaped disbelievingly at Miss James. She winked at

him. 'You going to keep playing or not?'

Mr French gave a wry smile. 'Thanks, but I've got enough bruises as it is. You carry on without me. There's something I have to do.' He turned around quickly and limped off after Noura.

22

Cough

Alfie hurried along the path through the forest. I mustn't stay away too long, he thought. Otherwise they'll notice I'm gone. All of a sudden he heard a strange coughing noise and stood still. Was there someone else in the forest? He looked around. Leaves rustled softly in the breeze and a squirrel ran away on a branch.

Alfie burst out laughing. It was that squirrel, he thought, quickly walking on.

'Do squirrels cough like people?' the voice in his head asked.

'Of course not, don't be an idiot,' Alfie mumbled. 'No one coughed. That was just the wind, or a crow with a sore throat or something.'

'Oh!' the voice in his head said. 'I thought it was a suspicious cough!'

But Alfie had decided to ignore the voice.

A bit further along, he saw something red in the undergrowth. 'Yes, look, there they are.' Shirt, jeans, socks, shoes. His coat was inside out and caught on a bush. His shirt was torn. In his thoughts he heard Tim's mother saying, 'Messy, messy. Always fold your clothes up neatly, Alfie. And try not to burst out of them when you turn into a werewolf.'

He pulled the plastic bag out of his pocket and quickly gathered up the clothes, putting all of them in the bag, except for the coat, which he put on.

And now back to the farm, thought Alfie.

Behind him, someone coughed. Alfie jumped.

'That's a suspicious cough,' said the voice in his head.

Very slowly Alfie turned around and found himself looking straight at a strange face. A boy was crouched half hidden in the bushes. Tall and skinny. A pointy face. Cropped hair. Big ears. His eyebrows joined together to form one thick, continuous stripe. The boy was at least two heads taller than Alfie and he looked a lot older too. Maybe sixteen or even seventeen.

The soup thief! was Alfie's first thought. The nosy parker who had peered in through the window.

The boy studied Alfie carefully. He held his head to one side and sniffed, puckering up his nose to do it. It was more snuffling than sniffing.

'What youse be looking for?'

Alfie looked at the boy in surprise.

'I, um, I was just looking for my clothes. They were here.' He gestured at the plastic bag and picked it up cautiously. 'I . . .'

The boy came out of the bushes and pointed at Alfie with an outstretched arm. The nail of his index finger was long and

sharp. Alfie could see dirt under the fingernail. All of his nails had thick black edges as if he'd been digging in the mud.

The boy actually looked dirty all over. His clothes were covered with sand, twigs and thistles. His coat and trousers looked as if they had exploded and been stuck back together with thread, string, staples, safety pins and sticky tape. It was an astonishing sight.

'Leo's knowing what youse be!' the boy said. 'Leo's smelling it the first time he seed you. Leo smells it he does, with his snozzler.'

Again the boy snuffled so hard that funny-looking wrinkles appeared on his nose, but Alfie didn't laugh.

The boy approached him menacingly. 'Leo be firster in this forest. Lots firsterer than you. Leo's wanting you goners from here.'

Alfie stepped back. He didn't understand. Who was this Leo the boy was talking about? And why did Leo want him to go away. If only Tim was here.

The boy came even closer, growled and bared his teeth. Then he patted himself on the chest. 'Leo be firster here.'

Oh, he's called Leo himself, thought Alfie. What a nutcase!

'Gets!' Leo shouted. 'And quicks-a-daisies, or Leo's biting you!' With a growl, he leapt forward. Alfie screamed.

23

Confused

'Hey, Alfie, there you are!'

Surprised, Alfie turned around. Noura was standing there and behind her stood Mr French. Alfie looked back at Leo, but Leo wasn't there any more. He'd disappeared as suddenly as if he had dissolved into thin air. Only the bushes were moving. Alfie turned his head left and right with a dazed look in his eyes. How had he done that?

'Are you OK, Alfie?' Mr French asked.

Alfie gave an absent-minded nod. 'Yes, I's fine. I mean, I'm fine. I thought that Leo . . .'

Mr French looked at Alfie thoughtfully. 'Leo? Who's Leo?'

Alfie shook his head. 'I . . . I don't know. There was someone here a minute ago. Someone called Leo. At least I thought there was. But I was wrong, I think.'

Noura took him by the arm. 'Poor Alfie. What are you doing walking around here by yourself with that plastic bag?' She looked in the bag. 'There are clothes in here! What are they for? Are you going somewhere?'

Oh, no! What am I supposed to say now, thought Alfie. 'Uh, just . . . spare clothes, in case I get dirty.'

Mr French looked at Noura. 'It seems to me Alfie is a bit confused. I'm glad you realized, Noura. And fortunately I was able to catch up to you. Come on, Alfie, let's go back. I'd rather not have my kids wandering around the forest alone.'

Noura took Alfie by the hand. It made him feel warm inside, but he felt a bit sad too. If Noura knew I was a werewolf, she wouldn't take me by the hand, he thought.

Noura gave his hand a little squeeze and smiled at him. Luckily, she doesn't know, thought Alfie.

'We're going to an old mill soon,' said Mr French. 'I'm sure you'll enjoy it. There's a bakery attached to the mill. They're going to let you make your own bread. Won't that be fun?'

Alfie nodded vaguely. He was thinking about Leo. What a strange boy. Why did he want to bite me? It's weird, but there was something familiar about him. Maybe that's why I didn't say anything to Mr French. Alfie shook his head. He didn't understand it at all. Suddenly he remembered something else. 'Sir, there's something I wanted to ask you.'

Mr French looked back.

'Can Rose come to the bakery with us? I know she's a pain sometimes, but I still feel sorry for her if she—'

Mr French smiled. 'I really wasn't going to leave her behind all by herself, Alfie. But it's nice of you to think of her.'

* * *

Up in a tree, hidden by the leaves, sat the soup thief. He watched the teacher and the children walk off, then used his nails to gouge deep lines in the bark. He picked a beetle out of a crack, held it up in the air and dropped it into his mouth. 'Leo be firster here,' he growled.

24

A Poor Old Man

Tim walked through the gate and into Green Park. It was quiet. The ducks were asleep on the water and the benches were empty. The mothers with prams had all gone home. The sun had almost set and it was getting dark.

Maybe I'll find him now, Tim thought, starting to feel a little dejected. He'd been searching for Grandpa Werewolf all day. He'd looked on all the streets and down all the lanes. He'd already been to Green Park twice, first in the morning and again in the afternoon.

It was in Green Park that Alfie had met his grandfather for the first time, but Tim was out of luck now. There was no sign of Alfie's grandpa. None, nothing, nada. Grandpa Werewolf lived faraway in a forest, where he was a wolf day and night. That was something that only very old werewolves could do, but although he had decided never to become human again, he sometimes missed the human world. Then he would put on his human clothes – a long coat, black gloves and a black hat – pull on boots and go into town for a few days. His favourite place was Green Park. It had lots of trees and bushes.

Grandpa Werewolf liked to watch people and, hidden in the bushes, he could relax for hours at a time, knowing he wouldn't frighten anyone. No one saw him. He made sure of that.

Alfie was the only person he had revealed himself to. Later he had got to know Tim and his parents as well.

But now I can't find him anywhere, thought Tim, just when I need him most. He wiped the sweat from his forehead. His skin was glowing, but at the same time he was getting cold shivers every now and then. Tim knew what that meant. He was still running a temperature. He should be home in bed.

Not yet! he thought. Just a little bit longer. If I find Grandpa Werewolf, everything will turn out fine. He'll take care of Alfie and then nothing will go wrong. But where is he?

'Grandpa!' he called. 'Grandpa Werewolf, are you here? I need to talk to you. It's urgent.' His voice boomed out across the silent park. All he heard in reply was the plaintive cry of a distant peacock. There was nobody else around. A duck took off with a flutter of wings. Tim stuck his hands deep into his pockets and shrugged. He was wasting his time. Grandpa Werewolf wasn't here. He was probably miles away in his own forest waiting for the full moon to rise.

Feeling miserable, Tim trudged towards the park exit. Alfie would have to manage by himself. There was no way round it. Tim felt his legs getting weaker by the second. He was boiling hot and freezing cold by turns. Now I have to try to make it home, he thought.

'Pssst . . . Hey, kid!'

Tim looked back in surprise. A man in a baggy coat was coming towards him. He was wearing a hat with a floppy brim.

Tim's heart leapt.

'Grandpa W—'

A horrible smell of booze wafted towards him. It wasn't Grandpa Werewolf at all. The eyes gleaming under the brim of the hat were completely different. Only now did Tim see the bottle sticking out of the coat pocket.

The man burped and grinned. 'So, sonny. You've got some money for a poor old man, haven't you?' He held out his hand.

Tim shrank

away from him. 'I haven't got anything, leave me alone.' He started feeling dizzy. The man's face came closer. Tim saw stubble and stumpy yellow teeth.

'Now now, you can be friendlier than that,' the man said. 'Have a look in your wallet. I'm sure you've got something to spare.'

His hand, as bony as a bird's claw, shot out and grabbed Tim by the shoulder.

'Let go!' Tim screamed. His legs had turned to spaghetti. The world was spinning. He could still smell the stinking booze and it was making him feel sick.

Then he heard an angry growl as something dark rushed down the path. The ducks started quacking loudly and Tim saw the man suddenly lift up off the ground.

25

Grandpa Werewolf

Tim could hardly believe his tired eyes. The strange man was being lifted up into the air. For a moment he looked like a propeller with his arms and legs swinging. Then he flew over the path and landed with a splash in the pond. That was the final straw for the ducks, who flew off, quacking angrily.

Tim found it hard to stay standing. The sky, the trees, the park, everything was spinning. The path was moving up and down as if Tim was standing on the deck of a ship. He saw the dark figure rocking back and forth in front of him on the path. The figure was leaning on a walking stick and now bent forward.

'Are you all right, Tim?'

Tim recognized the voice. The harsh sound. The raspy breathing. 'Grandpa Werewolf?' The next instant he collapsed.

The last thing he saw was a glimpse of the black wolf's head under the hat. Shining teeth. Gleaming eyes. Then nothing.

Tim's father was watching TV. He was wearing the wolf mask from the fancy-dress shop and the elephant tea cosy was on top of the TV. Sometimes I miss that tea cosy, he thought. It really was a lot more comfortable than this wolf mask. But I'm doing it for Alfie. I want to know how he feels when he's a werewolf. Maybe I'll understand it even better if I . . .

Dad slid down off the sofa, put his hands on the floor and started to crawl around the room. He sniffed the chairs, the table and the sofa. With his nose just above the carpet, he snuffled his way around the whole room until suddenly he bumped into a shoe. In the shoe there was a leg. Dad's eyes travelled up. Jeans. A jumper. A face.

Mum looked down at him from above. 'What are you doing now?'

'*Wrow!* I mean: I'm trying to be a werewolf. Like Alfie, see? So I'll know how he feels at full moon.'

Mum shook her head. 'That's very sweet of you. As long as you don't pee on the table leg! But to be honest, honey, you don't look very much like a wolf.'

'Really?' Dad's voice sounded sad and Mum realized that she had hurt his feelings. He was very sensitive.

'Well, a little bit,' she said. 'But have you heard from Tim? It's already dark.'

'He was home for a while, then he went out again. The poor boy couldn't relax. He had to find Grandpa Werewolf, he said.'

Just then the doorbell rang.

'Ah, that'll be him!' Mum walked into the hall and opened the front door, but immediately stepped back.

'Tim!' she said in a shocked voice. Her son was lying slumped in the arms of a dark figure in a black hat.

26

Not Safe

'Grandpa Werewolf! What happened? Come in, quickly.'

Grandpa Werewolf stepped into the house and carried Tim to the living room. 'Don't worry,' he growled. 'It's nothing serious. Tim has to go to bed, that's all.' He laid Tim on the sofa, then turned back to Mum with a stern expression. 'But why was he out looking for me when he has a temperature? Why was he calling my name in the park?'

He looked at Dad, who was just crawling out from under the table. 'And why is your husband wearing that funny-looking wolf mask?'

Dad held his head to one side for a moment and growled softly. 'I'm trying to be a werewolf,' he said with pride.

'Well, don't,' Grandpa Werewolf grunted. 'You look like an idiot. You only become a werewolf if it's in the family. Or if you get bitten by a real werewolf.'

Dad took off the wolf mask and sat there crestfallen. His face was bright red and sweaty and his hair was sopping wet.

'I was doing it for Alfie,' he mumbled.

'Ah, Alfie!' Grandpa cried. 'Where is my favourite grandson? I want to take him to the woods to run wild together. It's full moon tonight, so—'

'That's why we were looking for you,' Mum said. 'Alfie is already in the forest. With school. We wanted to ask if you could keep an eye out for him.'

Grandpa Werewolf sat down. He clamped the walking stick between his legs and laid his hat on his knee. Dad stared at Grandpa's black wolf's head jealously. Oh, if only I had a head like that, Dad thought, instead of this mask. Then I might feel like a real werewolf. He hurled the wolf mask into the corner of the room. Maybe Grandpa will bite me if I ask him to, he thought. Then I'd turn into a real werewolf. That would be fantastic. He coughed quietly.

'Ahem, there's something I'd like to ask.'

Grandpa Werewolf gave him a searching look that made Dad blush a little.

'If I asked you to, would you . . . I mean, maybe you could, um . . .'

'What are you getting at?' Mum said. 'Just tell Grandpa Werewolf what you want.'

Dad cleared his throat. 'I was wondering if, sometime, you could, maybe . . .'

He fell silent when Grandpa Werewolf fixed him with a scorching gaze. Dad shrunk. It was as if Grandpa Werewolf was looking deep into his soul. As if he knew everything Dad had ever wished or hoped and all his secret desires.

'No,' Grandpa Werewolf growled, banging

his walking stick down on the floor. 'Not now and not ever. Understood? And never ask me something like that again!'

Dad nodded silently, but Mum was completely baffled.

'What are you talking about?'

Grandpa Werewolf stared at Mum. He ran his tongue over his teeth.

'Nothing important. We were talking about my grandson, that's much more important. Where is Alfie?'

'Sulphur Forest,' Dad replied.

'What?' Grandpa Werewolf jumped up so fast he sent his chair clattering over backwards. 'He's in Sulphur Forest at full moon?'

Mum and Dad exchanged worried glances.

'He's not there by himself. His class and his teacher are there too.'

'That's irrelevant,' Grandpa snapped. 'It's not safe for Alfie in Sulphur Forest at full moon.'

Dad scratched his head nervously. 'Why not?'

Grandpa Werewolf grabbed his walking stick, squeezed his hat down on his head and strode out to the hall, stopping for a moment at the front door.

'What's wrong with Sulphur Forest?' Mum asked.

Grandpa Werewolf looked back and said one word, 'Leo!'

'Who's Leo?' Dad asked with surprise, but the hall was already empty. A cold wind blew in through the open door.

27

Staying Behind

Mr French and the children came back from the mill covered with white flour. It had been a very enjoyable afternoon. They had all got to bake their own bread. Noura had made a small loaf shaped like a heart and given it to Alfie. Of course, Alfie had given his loaf to Noura. It looked more like a banana, but Noura liked it anyway. Alfie had done his best.

By the time they got back to the farm it was already late in the afternoon.

'OK, kids,' Mr French said. 'Go and freshen

up. Brush that flour off your clothes and stick your heads under a tap. Miss James has made pancakes and in one hour we're going into the forest.'

Alfie went up to Mr French. 'Sir, is it OK if I stay at the farm tonight?'

Mr French looked surprised. 'What's all this about, Alfie? Don't you want to go into the woods for a mega-thrilling, super-scary, mysterious stroll through the gloom?'

Alfie hesitated for a moment. 'I don't really feel that well. It might be better if I stayed at the farmhouse. I don't like dark forests much anyway.'

Mr French rubbed his chin. 'I don't think that's such a good idea, Alfie. Everyone's going. Miss James too, I'm afraid. I'd rather not leave you behind by yourself. You never know.'

Just then Noura stepped forward. Alfie hadn't noticed her standing behind him, but she had heard the whole conversation.

'Sir, I can stay behind with Alfie. I think it would be lonely here all alone.'

Alfie looked at Noura, stunned. Alone with her at the farm at full moon? That was definitely a bad idea. If Noura stayed behind with him, she would find out that he was a werewolf and that was the last thing he wanted. If only Tim was here. He always had answers for everything, but now Alfie had to solve his own problems. He could see Mr French thinking deeply.

'Well, that does change things,' he said. 'Maybe . . .'

Alfie's mind raced. He had no choice. He had to go on the walk after all and then slip away from the group without being noticed when he started to change.

'Um, suddenly I feel as right as rain!' he said, trying to look cheerful. He did a little jig. 'Look, fit as a fiddle.' He stretched his arms and legs. 'See. I'll be perfectly fine to come along.'

Mr French was flabbergasted. He shrugged. 'OK, great, we've solved that one then. But are you sure you feel all right? You were acting a bit funny earlier this afternoon too.

You're not feeling homesick, are you? You're not thinking of sneaking off home?'

'No,' Alfie blurted. 'No way. I think this trip is cool. And I really want to go on the forest walk. At least, as long as we don't stay away too long.'

'OK,' said Mr French. 'I'm glad you're feeling better and don't worry. We're not going to be out walking all evening. We might even be back before it gets properly dark.' Mr French went into the farmhouse.

Noura looked a bit glum. 'Don't you like being with me?' she asked.

'I do, I like it a lot,' Alfie said. 'But I didn't want you to miss out on the forest walk because of me. That's why I'm coming after all.'

Noura started to beam. 'So you're doing it for me! How sweet. I bet it's going to be a lovely evening with a beautiful full moon.'

She didn't notice the wrinkle appearing on Alfie's brow.

'You're the nicest boy I know, Alfie Span. This afternoon you stuck up for Rose too. I thought that was really fabulous.'

Alfie hardly heard a word Noura said. He was looking up at the treetops. Some stars had already come out in the sky. Yes, he thought, a full moon.

28

A Screw Loose?

Making an enormous racket, the hunter roared up on his motorbike, with the beam of his headlight zigzagging between the trees. Like a dark veil the twilight hung over the farm.

The hunter skidded to a halt, throwing up a cloud of sand that rained down on Mr French and the children.

'You're ready, eh?'

Mr French brushed the sand off his clothes and shook it out of his hair. He cleared his throat, spitting out a brown glob, then said,

'Yes, we're ready,' in a sandy voice. 'We've just had a delicious meal. Miss James made pancakes. Surprisingly delicious pancakes, in fact. Then we all freshened up.'

Miss James blushed.

Mr French shook some more sand off the sleeve of his coat.

'Maybe that freshening up wasn't such a good idea,' Miss James said. 'I'm already covered with sand again.'

Grinning, the hunter climbed off his motorbike. 'That's life in the great outdoors, eh?'

He was wearing a hunting cap under his helmet and he had a hunting rifle slung over his back. He swung the rifle around and took it in his hands. 'My friend and I are ready too.' He stroked the gleaming, polished weapon and kissed it, winking at the children.

'Yuck, this guy is such a creep,' Noura said, squeezing Alfie's arm so hard her nails pressed into his skin. Alfie smiled bravely and didn't flinch. He was a bit worried. Not very worried, but a bit. He hoped the walk wouldn't last too long.

Mr French coughed. 'Um, Mr Bucket, is that really necessary?'

'What do you mean?'

'That, um, thing. That gun. Do you really need to bring it along? We're only going for a walk with the children.'

The hunter looked at Mr French, blinked, shook his head and gave a deep sigh. 'Listen carefully, Mr Teacher. We're going into the forest, eh?'

Mr French nodded.

'And you know who lives in the forest?'

Mr French hesitated a moment. 'I'm not sure what you're getting at.'

The hunter scowled. 'You know the song the three little pigs sing, eh?'

Mr French gave the hunter a despairing look. He was starting to worry that Hunter Sam hadn't been such a good choice. The man definitely had a screw loose.

Alfie fidgeted impatiently. When were they going to get started? The longer they dawdled, the earlier the full moon would appear.

The hunter hummed the tune of 'Who's Afraid of the Big Bad Wolf?' looking at Mr French and the children expectantly. *'Hmmm-hmm-hm of the hmmm-hmm-hm—'* He flapped his hand impatiently. No one said a word.

'Are we going now, sir?' Alfie asked.

'What kind of school is this?' Hunter Sam shouted. 'Any nincompoop knows that song. Big bad wolves live in forests.' He held his gun up for all to see. 'But I'm not afraid. And why not? Because my friend the gun is coming with us, you understand, eh? Any more questions?'

No one spoke and everyone stared at Hunter Sam.

Only Rose whispered quietly to herself, 'Big bad wolf. The big bad stupid wolf. I knew it!'

Alfie was starting to get nervous. 'Sir, are we going now or what?'

Mr French didn't seem to have heard him. He was staring at Hunter Sam with a dazed expression. I've made a mistake, he thought. This guy is mad, he's a maniac, an escaped lunatic, a headcase with a hunting licence. But I can't send him packing now. The children are looking forward to a walk in the forest.

'Good, we can finally get started then, eh?' Hunter Sam asked, slinging the gun back over his shoulder. 'It's already dark. In the forest under the trees you can't see a thing. You have your torches with you, hopefully, eh?' He pulled an enormous torch out from under his belt and switched it on. The beam of light was as wide as a door.

Mr French looked at Miss James, who nodded and handed out the torches. Six tiny torches with skinny little beams of light. The children had to share them out down the line. They were going to be walking in twos. Noura got one of the torches. She was walking next to Alfie.

Behind her, Rose grumbled, 'Why does Noura get one of those stupid torches and I don't?'

'Stop moaning, Rose,' Mr French said.
'We're off. You should be glad you're coming
at all.'

They flicked their torches on and
headed off.

29

Werewolf Itch

The long line of children followed Hunter Sam into the dark forest with Mr French at the front and Miss James at the back. The light from the torches cast ghostly shadows under the trees.

'Stay together,' Mr French called. 'I don't want to lose anyone now.'

Miss James suddenly appeared beside him, hooking her arm into his. 'I'll make sure you don't lose me, Roger.'

Sniggers went up from the children who were close enough to hear.

'She wants a kiss, sir,' Vincent whispered.

Mr French shuddered and shook Miss James off, as if she was something slimy. 'Miss James, what are you doing here? You're supposed to be last in line. Don't you have any sense of responsibility? Who's keeping an eye on the children at the back? You have to bring up the rear.'

With a red face, Miss James hurried back to the end of the line. Mr French whistled through his teeth.

'Pffff,' he mumbled. 'Why does she act so silly? She's actually quite nice and she makes fantastic pancakes, but . . .'

Vincent winked at him. 'You just missed getting a big, fat kiss, sir.'

Mr French tousled Vincent's hair. 'Watch out she doesn't give you a kiss, Vincent. You might turn into a big fat frog.'

Meanwhile Hunter Sam was leading the way at a smart pace, constantly humming 'Who's Afraid of the Big Bad Wolf?' Alfie was walking next to Noura.

'It's exciting, isn't it, walking in the dark

like this?' Noura said. Alfie nodded without really thinking, keeping his eyes fixed on the dark sky. Between the treetops he could already see a few twinkling stars. And the moon was vaguely visible as well. He scratched his head. Uh-oh!

Was that an ordinary itch or was it a werewolf itch? Hunter Sam had started singing now, over and over again, telling everyone he wasn't afraid.

Alfie scratched his neck. His cheeks had started getting itchy too. Suddenly Noura was holding the torch just in front of his face.

'Are you enjoying yourself, Alfie? You're so quiet.'

Quickly Alfie turned his head away, hoping Noura hadn't looked too closely. Maybe the hair was already growing on his cheeks.

'It's OK,' he said. 'But you shouldn't shine the torch in my eyes. You've blinded me.'

'Oh, sorry,' Noura said, turning the torch away from his face.

'It's no big deal,' he said.

'You sure there's nothing wrong?' Noura asked in a worried voice. She studied him carefully. Suddenly she shone the torch at Alfie's face again.

'Alfie, just turn your head.'

All of a sudden Noura screamed at the top of her voice . . .

30

Beetle

'What is it? What is it?' Mr French rushed up.

Everyone looked at Noura and Alfie. Noura pointed at Alfie's face. 'Th-th-there!' She was still pointing the torch at Alfie. The beam of light danced over his face. Alfie groaned silently with misery. I've had it! he thought. Everyone will see the hair on my cheeks. Now they will all know. If only Tim was here. This would never have happened.

Mr French hurried up to Alfie and stared hard at his face. 'Oh, I see. That's nothing to worry about, Alfie. Stay still for a second.'

He reached out with one hand. Alfie shrunk away.

'Stop moving,' Mr French said. 'Otherwise I can't grab the little monster.'

'Monster? What monster?' Alfie asked in a hoarse voice.

'An enormous beetle,' Noura shrieked. 'It's sitting on your forehead. A scary monster, all black and shiny, with wriggly legs. Can't you feel it? It must have fallen off a tree.'

'I did feel a bit of an itch,' Alfie said. 'But I thought . . .'

He put a hand up to his cheek, which was as soft and smooth as a baby's bottom. Thank goodness. It hadn't been the werewolf itch at all. There was nothing going on. Alfie was overcome by a deep sense of relief. What did he care if a beetle was sitting on his forehead! It could be an elephant for all he cared!

Mr French peered at Alfie's head with an expression of disgust. 'It really is a scary little creature. I don't know exactly what kind of beetle it is, but it's a whopper.'

By this time Hunter Sam had come to have

a look as well. He raised his gun to his shoulder.

'Ooh, those beetles are dangerous, eh? One bite and you are instantly paralysed. Then you turn green and your hair falls out. Shall I blow it away, eh? I can do it, no problem!'

For a moment Mr French forgot to be polite. 'Go away, you idiot. I'm not having you shoot at one of my kids!'

Hunter Sam stalked off. 'Have it your own way,' he mumbled. 'I only offered to help, eh?'

With one swipe of his hand, Mr French flicked the beetle off Alfie's forehead. It landed on the ground in front of him and scuttled off on its wriggly legs.

Hunter Sam was getting impatient. 'Can we carry on now? I don't have all night.'

The procession moved on.

'Where are we now, sir?' Noura asked.

Mr French looked around. Trees in all directions. All looking exactly the same.

'No idea, Noura. But Hunter Sam knows his way around.'

Alfie looked up. He could sense something. It was as if something was moving in the trees. As if something was creeping from branch to branch through the leaves. Jumping from tree to tree. Something heavy keeping pace with them above their heads.

'When are we going back, sir?' he asked.

'Soon, Alfie. Just be patient.'

Suddenly the trees were further apart, giving them a clear view of the sky. Bright stars and a big, round moon lit up a clearing in the forest. All of the trees had been cut down and there were a few trunks lying on the ground. Alfie stepped back into the shade of the surrounding trees.

'We'll rest here,' Hunter Sam said. 'You can sit on those tree trunks. There's room for everyone, eh? Then I'll tell you a ghost story. And after that I'll take you back, eh?'

Mr French raised one eyebrow. 'A ghost story? Are you sure? What kind of ghost story?'

'A scary ghost story,' Hunter Sam said. 'Modern youngsters like horror stories, eh? I read that in the newspaper. So I have a fantastic horror story. It really happened.

Here in this forest, eh?'

'Is it an appropriate story?' Mr French asked. 'It's actually time we were heading back. It's past the children's bedtime.'

'Don't be soft,' Hunter Sam grinned. 'Without me you won't find the way back anyway. And I'm not going until I've told my story.'

Mr French gave a very deep sigh. He trusted Hunter Sam about as far as he could throw him. The man had no idea at all when it came to kids.

Reluctantly, Mr French walked over to one of the tree trunks and sat down. If he tells a gruesome murder story, I'll punch him in the mouth! Mr French thought. Immediately he was shocked that he could even think such a thing. It was terrible! This Hunter Sam character made him feel simply murderous. He blushed and looked around. Fortunately he'd only thought it. Nobody had heard it. The children were already sitting on the tree trunks.

'Oh, how nice of you to come and sit next

to me,' Miss James whispered. Astonished, Mr French looked to the side.

'What? Oh, that was by accident. You see, I didn't want to sit too close to Hunter Sam. I'm worried I'll go for his throat if he starts acting weird.'

Miss James gave Mr French an odd look. 'Oh?' she said. 'You really are a wild animal, Roger. I like that.'

Mr French blushed.

Hunter Sam started telling his story. 'Long ago in this forest there lived a gruesome, spooky chewing-gum monster. It had grown from all the little bits of chewing gum that people spat out when they were walking through the forest.'

Ahmed yawned. 'Pfft, what kind of horror story's this?'

Mr French smiled with relief. 'I don't have to hit him now at least. My children are used to stories from *The Horror Bus*. This Bucket guy doesn't have a clue.'

Alfie stood under the trees while the others

listened to Hunter Sam's story. He stared numbly at the full moon, which was shining white and bright in the sky and hanging right over the clearing. It's too late! he thought. I can feel that it's going to happen again. The moonlight oozed over his skin. His face, his arms, his legs – every part of him started itching.

31

Hide!

Alfie looked down at his hands. White hair was spreading over them rapidly. This time it was real – werewolf itch – and there was no stopping it. Alfie didn't hesitate for a second; he stepped back into the darkness.

'Alfie, you coming?' he heard Noura call softly.

No! thought Alfie. No, no, no! She mustn't see me like this. He started to run away from the clearing where Noura and the others were sitting. He didn't look where he was going. He just kept running.

Dumb, dumb, dumb! he thought. I should have known. Stupid, stupid, stupid! I shouldn't have come on the forest walk. Idiot, idiot, idiot! I should have gone home with Dad. I knew that it would be full moon again. Why was I so pig-headed?

'Because you wanted to join in with the others,' the voice in his head interrupted. 'So stop moaning. Just make sure no one sees you.'

'Easy for you to say,' Alfie growled.

Panting, he leapt over a fallen tree. His tongue was hanging out of his mouth. All at once he felt like sitting down right where he was. He didn't have the energy to take another step. He was tired. He couldn't be bothered. It was all so pointless. What's more his shoes were pinching terribly and his clothes were way too tight. His neck hair was bulging out of his collar.

He sat down on a stump and leant his head on his forepaws. Why did I think no one would notice? I just wanted to have a nice time with Noura, but now I have to run away again. It will always be like this. Whenever it starts to be fun, I'll have to run away. Because I'm not normal like all the other kids.

If only Tim was here! How many times had he thought that by now? But Tim wasn't here. There was no one to comfort him. Alfie raised his face to the moon and howled. Two gleaming streams ran out of his eyes and down over his muzzle. He sniffed and howled again.

Maybe the others would hear him. What do I care? thought Alfie. They'll probably think it's a real wolf. And then they'll stay away. Anyway, I am a real wolf. A danger to the neighbourhood. A burden to Tim and his family. He hung his head. In the moonlight the tear that fell from his eye looked silver.

Suddenly he heard footsteps hurrying up behind him. Someone was coming. Shocked, Alfie looked around. The footsteps were close by. A beam of light pierced the bushes. Hide, thought Alfie. Quick, I have to . . . He looked left, he looked right.

Where could he go? The next instant Noura came running up.

She stood there panting and shaking twigs and leaves out of her hair. 'Alfie, what . . .' Then Noura fell silent.

32

Go Away!

For a few seconds Alfie sat perfectly still while Noura stood there staring at him. Then he moved, bringing his arms up over his head and bending forward until his snout was almost between his knees, trying to screw himself up into a ball, wishing he could just disappear.

'Go away!' he growled. 'Please. Just go away. Nobody's allowed to see me!'

Alfie stayed sitting there, bent over and not saying a word, not daring to look up at Noura. Maybe she'd start to scream or run away as fast as she could. Either way, she'd be terrified and never want to see him again. He waited. Not a leaf rustled. Not a twig snapped. Where was Noura? Had she run away already? Or fainted perhaps? Had she gone to get the rest of them?

Alfie was still too scared to look up and made a growling, sobbing noise. His shoulders jolted. Suddenly he felt a hand on his neck, a warm hand gently stroking him.

'Alfie,' Noura said. 'Don't cry.'

Pointy fingertips tickled his head. Alfie raised his shoulders fearfully with his whole body trembling.

'Alfie, look at me.'

Alfie shook his head.

'Come on, look at me.'

'I'm too scared.'

Again Noura's fingers stroked his coat until finally Alfie raised his head. His wet eyes were gleaming. Now she would start screaming.

'Oh, poor Alfie,' Noura said in a sweet, gentle voice. She took his head between her two hands. 'What is this? What happened to you?'

'*Wrow*,' he whimpered softly. 'I . . . I'm a werewolf. I have been since I turned seven. I can't help it. Each month at full moon I turn into a wolf. Usually three nights in a row. This is the second night.'

'Oh,' said Noura. 'So last night you were . . .'

Alfie nodded. 'It's in my family. My grandpa is a werewolf too.' He hung his head. 'So now you know. Go tell the others. Tell them I'm a monster.'

'Never! What do you take me for? You're not a monster! And you needn't think I'd betray your secret. Not to anyone! Poor Alfie. Is this why you've been acting strange the whole time? Now I understand. You must have been so scared.'

Alfie finally dared to raise his head. He looked into the brown eyes with the golden speckles. '*Wrow*? But, um, don't you think I'm horrific? I'm a wild animal. A drooling wolf. I pee on trees. I devour chickens in my free time!'

Noura smiled. 'Is that all! I know people who do things that are much worse than that. And they're not even werewolves. What's more,' she grabbed Alfie's head again, 'I think you're a very cute wolf.'

She planted a quick kiss on the top of Alfie's head and a feeling of enormous happiness surged through him. Noura wrapped her arms around his neck. 'You're just a nice big cuddly toy. You feel just like my teddy bear.'

'*Wrow*.'

Alfie had a tremendous urge to wag his tail. He panted hard with his tongue hanging out of his mouth. This must be what a dog feels like when its owner hugs it.

He looked up at the sky and saw a magnificent moon, round and full like a giant ping-pong ball, a moon that made him want to howl for joy.

'Ouch!' Noura suddenly shouted.

'What's wrong?' growled Alfie, startled.

There was blood on Noura's neck. He had been so overjoyed, he had bitten her.

33

Leo's Forest

Stupid, clumsy werewolf! flashed through his head and he immediately started whimpering with misery. 'Oh, Noura. I didn't mean to, um, it was—'

'Shhh, hush,' Noura consoled him. 'It was only a nip. It doesn't hurt.'

'*Wrow*, are you sure?'

Noura nodded and wiped the blood away with a tissue.

There were teeth marks visible on her neck and she was still bleeding. Alfie felt really awful, but the next instant they heard a loud rustling above their heads. Branches snapped and leaves floated down. Then something big fell out of the sky, landing right in front of them. Something with arms and legs. A boy. He banged down on the ground and jumped up immediately. It was a tall, skinny boy with a pointy face, cropped hair, big ears and one thick, joined-up eyebrow. His jeans and coat were held together by string, sticky tape and staples. Leo!

The boy looked at Alfie, curled his upper lip and growled. 'Leo warnded you. This be Leo's forest. Youse had to go. Now Leo's biting you!'

Alfie stood dead still opposite Leo. Noura grabbed Alfie's paw and looked at the big boy in terror. 'Who's he?' she whispered. 'And why is he wearing those silly clothes? Do you know him?'

Alfie didn't take his eyes off the boy. 'That's Leo,' he growled. 'I don't know him. I don't know what he wants from me.'

'Out of the ways!' Leo snarled at Noura.

'I's gonna bites him.'

Immediately Alfie leapt in front of Noura, growling menacingly. 'You should leave while you can, Leo. Otherwise I'll bite you. I'm a wolf!'

Leo stared at Alfie for a moment, then started laughing. He bent over double and slapped his knees with his hands. Leo shrieked with laughter.

'What's wrong with him?' Noura asked. 'What's he laughing at?'

'I don't know,' growled Alfie.

Leo was still bent over with laughter. When he straightened up again, his eyes were bright yellow. 'Youse call that a wolf?' he growled. 'Don't make Leo laugh! That be no wolf.'

In one go Leo changed. He grew bigger. He grew wider. His big ears turned pointy. Suddenly he was hairy all over. His face stretched into a snout and his mouth turned into two jaws full of sharp teeth. His hands changed to paws. His feet burst out of his shoes. His clothes ripped open, tearing from top to bottom. Strips of material flew off in all directions. Staples, safety pins and bits of string shot off.

'So that's why he wears those silly clothes,' Noura whispered. 'He keeps bursting out of them.'

'Wow, I almost never do that,' growled Alfie. 'At least, not so much.' There was admiration in his voice.

Standing in front of them was an enormous grey wolf, at least twice as big as Alfie. He was so gigantic, his body seemed to block out the moon. His eyes glowed. His teeth flashed. His voice sounded like thunder. 'This be a wolf! Leo be a wolf. And now he does more than just biteses. Now Leo's eating little wolfie up. Every last bits. All his little teeths and nailses. His whole caboodles. Little wolfie should've listened to Leo. Leo warnded him.'

The enormous werewolf stretched and roared at the moon. His claws shone like daggers in the moonlight. The trees seemed to tremble and Alfie cringed with fear. He didn't stand a chance against such an enormous wolf. And Tim wasn't there to come up with a clever plan.

Suddenly Noura jumped in front of him. 'Go away, you big bully. Leave Alfie alone. Otherwise . . .'

The big wolf looked down on her with a sneer. 'Other whys . . . Other whats? Out of the way, smidget.' With a single swipe, Leo brushed Noura aside, sending her rolling over the ground and crashing into a tree two or three metres away. Noura stayed lying there, dead still.

'Beast,' Alfie growled, throwing himself at Leo.

'Youse right!' Leo roared. 'Leo be a brutes of a beast!' His claws shot out and he grabbed Alfie by the scruff of his neck, lifting him up as if he was as light as a feather. In the same instant, a voice rang through the forest.

'Leo, stop that!'

34

Cousins

Leo was still holding Alfie up in the air. Surprised he turned his enormous head. 'Huh? Who be calling Leo's name?'

Alfie kicked furiously in an attempt to break free. His legs thrashed wildly but Leo had no trouble at all holding him up in the air. He gave Alfie a shake.

'Stop wriggling, youse,' Leo growled. 'Be a bit patient, please. Leo's eating you up soon enoughs. First Leo's wanting to know who be calling his name.'

'Shame on you, Leo,' the same voice called.

'Let him go this instant.'

Alfie was astonished to see a familiar figure approaching on the path. Hat, long raincoat, walking stick . . .

Alfie recognized him immediately.

'Grandpa Werewolf!' he shouted, wriggling again.

'What's Leo told you?'

But Alfie was too excited, with joy this time. Grandpa Werewolf was coming. He was saved!

Panting, the old wolf came closer, his hat crooked on his head. He waved his walking stick in the air, then pointed it at Leo. Alfie's courage sank into his werewolf paws. Next to Leo, Grandpa looked very puny. The old werewolf would be helpless against the enormous young werewolf.

'Put him down, Leo,' Grandpa snapped. 'Now!'

To Alfie's astonishment, Leo obeyed immediately, gently putting Alfie down on the ground. Noura scrambled back up and ran over to Alfie.

Leo's mighty forelegs hung limp alongside his body. He looked at Grandpa Werewolf. 'Grandpa be angry?'

Alfie was totally confused. Leo must know Grandpa. More than that: Leo called Grandpa 'Grandpa'.

Grandpa Werewolf glared at Leo for a moment with a fiery look in his eyes. Then he reached out with one paw and the glow in his eyes dimmed. He scratched Leo between the ears. He had to stand on his toes and stretch up high to do it.

'No, I'm not angry at you. But don't ever try to eat my grandson again.'

Leo's eyes turned glassy. He looked at Alfie, then at Grandpa Werewolf, then back at Alfie. He did it a few times. His mouth dropped, his tongue rolled out.

'Little werewolf be Grandpa's grandson too?'

Now it was Alfie's turn to be astonished. 'Too? Is Leo your grandson too?'

Grandpa Werewolf nodded and smiled with a grin so wide it showed every last one of his teeth. 'That's right, you're both my grandsons. You're cousins!'

Leo looked at Alfie. 'Cousin!' he roared. 'I be your cousin, youse be my cousin.' He spread his forelegs, then lifted Alfie up again, this time almost crushing him in a warm hug.

Then he put Alfie back down and started bawling. Big fat tears ran down his muzzle and splashed on to Alfie's head. 'Leo be sorry! He's close to eating up his own little werewolf cuz. Forgives him, forgives him. Leo be sore-fully, sore-fully, sorry.'

Alfie stood there a little awkwardly. He wasn't sure what to do. Should he comfort the wolf that had been going to eat him just a moment before?

'I feel a bit sorry for him, don't you?' whispered Noura.

Alfie hesitated, then stretched out a paw. 'Um, Leo, I forgive you, OK? I—'

He didn't get a chance to say another word. Suddenly there was an enormous racket as all kinds of figures emerged from the undergrowth. Leading the way was Hunter Sam with his super torch. Behind him came Mr French, Miss James and the other kids. Everyone was there.

Oh no! thought Alfie. Too late. Now they can all see me. He tried to get away from Hunter Sam's bright light, hiding behind Noura, but the hunter summed up the situation in a glance. 'A-ha! I told you, eh? Wolves. Hen-killers!'

'Cool!' shouted Vincent. 'This is a lot more exciting than Hunter Sam's tired old ghost story.'

The hunter panted with excitement. 'Now you're glad my friend's here eh? Now I can blast away after all!'

He raised his gun and took aim.

'Stop!' screamed Noura.

35

Bang!

There was a loud bang. A flame shot out of the barrel of the rifle. Alfie and Noura both jumped with fright and horror. Leo let out an ear-splitting screech, disappeared into the bushes with one enormous leap and ran off yelping.

'Eh, too bad,' said Hunter Sam. 'I only hit his ear, I think.'

Quickly, he reloaded his rifle.

'Wait,' Mr French shouted. 'Wait! No more shooting! Can't you see that's one of our kids right there. Next thing you'll hit Noura.'

'Oh, really?' screamed Hunter Sam. 'What about that funny-looking dressed-up wolf, eh? I've seen that one before in my henhouse. Just like that big grey one, eh? Except that time the white one wasn't wearing any clothes.'

Mr French scratched his head. He saw a small, white wolf dressed in Alfie's clothes. He saw Noura. And he saw a strange character in a long raincoat, with a hat on. He looked like a wolf too, an old wolf with a hat and a walking stick.

'I wouldn't do that,' the old wolf said. 'I wouldn't shoot at these innocent children.'

Mr French's head started to spin. A talking wolf with a coat and a hat!

'Noura, what is this all about?' Mr French asked. 'Can you explain it to me?'

Before Noura could answer, Rose stepped forward, pointing at Alfie.

'That's it!' she shouted. 'That's the stupid white wolf that was in the boys' toilets. I told you. I knew it. That stupid wolf almost scared me to death. Go on, shoot it, you stupid hunter. Shoot it!'

Hunter Sam put his gun up to his shoulder.

'No!' Mr French shouted.

'Oh, yes,' Hunter Sam muttered. 'Yes! I'm going to shoot that white wolf right between the eyes. If you ask me it's eaten up one of your pupils, eh? And then it put on his clothes.'

'What kind of drivel is that?' Mr French said. 'Wolves don't do things like that.'

Hunter Sam wasn't listening. He squeezed one eye shut and aimed at Alfie.

'No, don't!' Noura screamed, jumping in front of Alfie.

'Out of the way, girlie, or I'll hit you too, eh?'

'Not on your nelly, buster!' Mr French shouted. 'You've fired your last shot around here.' He clenched one fist, pulled his arm all the way back, then sent his fist whizzing through the air at maximum speed. It was like a rocket rushing in from outer space to land with a bang on Hunter Sam's chin.

Hunter Sam's legs buckled. His eyes rolled back in their sockets. He fell like a tree that's been cut. The rifle went off with an enormous bang, shooting up into the sky. Hunter Sam didn't make another noise. All the children stared speechlessly at their teacher.

'Wow!' said Vincent, in a voice full of admiration.

Miss James was all aflutter. She skipped around Mr French. She patted him on the shoulder. She pinched him on the cheek. 'Oh, Roger, that was so brave! What a fantastic punch. Wow! You're a real hero. I

feel like giving you a big kiss.'

'It was nothing,' Mr French said, blushing slightly. He blew on his knuckles, which had turned bright red. Hopefully nothing was broken, but he could worry about that later. He still didn't understand what was going on.

He walked over to Noura and pointed at the white, dressed-up wolf. 'Noura, who or what is that? And why is it wearing Alfie's clothes?'

Noura gave Alfie a confused look. She didn't want to give away his secret. 'Um, how can I put it, sir? This wolf here is . . .'

36

Mad?

'Alfie,' said another voice.

'What . . . what's going on now?' Mr French asked.

Three wolves stepped out of the bushes.

'This little wolf is definitely Alfie,' one of the three announced. Anyone could see they weren't

173

real wolves. They were wearing bathrobes with little wolves on them, they had on grey gloves and they were wearing wolf slippers.

The biggest of the three grabbed his wolf mask and pulled it off. It was Tim's father. Then the other two took off their masks as well.

'Mum!' shouted Alfie. 'Tim!' He ran up to Tim and threw his arms around him. 'You're here at last. I wished for it so many times.'

Tim's mother hugged Alfie.

'Can someone finally tell me what this

is all about?' Mr French asked. 'I don't understand anything any more.'

'Neither do we!' shouted the children from Years 3 and 4. 'We understand even less than that. Why does Alfie look like a wolf?' They all looked at Alfie, who felt rather uncomfortable. Tim's father walked over to Mr French.

'Take it easy, Mr French. No need for panic. I'll explain exactly what it's all about.'

Alfie held his breath. He didn't get it. Why was Tim's father going to betray his secret? Had he gone mad? Alfie turned to Tim with a helpless look on his face. Tim smiled. 'Don't worry,' he whispered. 'Dad has worked it all out perfectly.'

Dad gave a little cough. 'You see, it's like this. We're a family with traditions. And we like unusual things. Especially me, if I say so myself.' Tim's father winked at his wife, who blew him a kiss.

'For instance, I'm fond of wandering around with a tea cosy on my head,' Dad went on. 'A biscuit tin is another possibility, or a flower pot. I think high heels are cool too, sometimes. As long as it's different from usual. Sometimes I even wear a dress or clogs or a cute little bathing suit. You're familiar with that kind of thing, aren't you?'

Mr French stared speechlessly at Tim's father and shook his head.

'No?' Tim's father said. 'Oh well, in any case, I like things to be different. And that's why we hold a wolf day every now and then.'

'A what?' asked Mr French.

37

Wolf Day

'A wolf day,' Dad said with a smile. 'When we all dress up as wolves, mostly at full moon. We put our wolf masks on and pull on our wolf slippers and then we run wild in the woods. Or sit on a hill and howl at the moon.'

'Traditions?' Mr French mumbled.

Dad nodded. 'Exactly, Mr French. Traditions.' He looked at Tim and Mum and clicked his fingers. 'Give it to them, sweethearts.'

Mum and Tim put on their wolf masks,

looked up at the moon and launched into an ear-piercing howl. They did dance steps to go along with it and clicked their fingers in time to the howling.

The children from Years 3 and 4 screamed with laughter. Most of them covered their ears with their hands. Others just pointed and almost wet themselves. Alfie got a lump in his throat. He could see how Mum and Tim were doing their very best to make fools of themselves.

And they're doing it all for me! he thought.

Dad gave a sign and Mum and Tim stopped. Quickly, they took off their wolf masks. They both had red sweaty faces from all the exertion.

'Magnificent, don't you think?' Dad said.

Mr French stared at Dad as if he was totally crazy.

Dad smiled back cheerfully. 'And you haven't even heard Grandpa yet. He's much better at it. Would you like to hear him too?'

Dad pointed at Grandpa Werewolf who was watching the scene with a big grin on his snout. He waved at Mr French with his walking stick.

Mr French waved back hesitantly. 'No, no, I don't need to hear any more. It's all very convincing.'

'Alfie and Grandpa have the best outfits,' Dad continued. 'They've got real wolf suits. To be honest, I'm a bit jealous of them. The zips don't even show.'

'Zips?' mumbled Mr French.

'Yes, the zips of their wolf suits, of course,' Dad sniggered. 'Or did you think maybe they were real wolves? Feel free to have a look. Would you like to feel Alfie's coat?'

Mr French wavered, then took a step towards Alfie.

38

Fibs

Suddenly Alfie felt horribly frightened.

Mr French smiled. 'No, that's all right. I understand now. Last night Alfie was trying on his suit in the boys' toilets. And then Rose came in and thought he was a real wolf. That's why she got such a fright, of course.' Mr French screwed up one eye and stared hard at Alfie. 'I must say, that suit looks so real!'

Alfie sighed with relief and looked at Tim. 'Your father's great at fibbing,' he whispered. 'It's fantastic that he thought all this up to save me.'

Tim looked at him for a moment. 'What did you expect?' he whispered. 'He loves you! We all do.'

Mr French ran his fingers through his hair, shook his head and squeezed his chin with one hand. He stared at Tim's father. 'But, um, what are you doing here tonight? If you don't mind my asking.'

Dad burst out laughing. 'I thought you understood. I'm very sorry, but we've come to pick up Alfie. Our wolf day just happens to be important to us as a family. It's a cosy get-together. Just like Christmas, if you know what I mean. But then without a Christmas tree, of course. And on an occasion like that we can't do without Alfie. He is just as important to us as Tim.'

Mr French pondered for a moment. 'Couldn't you have thought of that before? Before Alfie came away on the school trip with us, I mean.'

Dad turned the wolf mask around in his hands. 'You're right, Mr French. You are absolutely right, but we just didn't realize. You see, Tim forgot to tear the page off the week planner. And as a result we didn't know that it was already full moon this week. We were a week behind, you see?'

Wow, that's smart, thought Alfie. Dad's story is partly true.

Mr French thought for a long time, rubbing his nose and staring into space. Everyone was quiet.

'Um, it's quite an exceptional story you're telling me here, but fine. I wouldn't want to get in the way of such an important family celebration. Alfie, you can go with your family. I'll see you back at school the day after tomorrow.'

'Thanks, sir,' Alfie growled.

Mum, Dad and Tim put their wolf masks back on.

'We'll be off then,' Dad said. 'Grandpa Werew— I mean, Grandpa, where . . . did we park the car? Shall we go?'

Grandpa Werewolf stared thoughtfully at Noura.

'Grandpa, are you coming?' Dad asked again.

'What? What? Oh, yes, I'm coming, that's right.'

All of a sudden the old werewolf seemed confused. He gazed at Noura one last time, then followed the family. Alfie waved goodbye to Mr French and Years 3 and 4.

'I'll see you the day after tomorrow,' he growled softly to Noura.

She smiled sweetly and blew him a kiss, copying Tim's mother.

'We'll see you the day after tomorrow, Alfie,' called Mr French. 'We'll take care of your sleeping bag and stuff. That's a cool costume you've got there, really. That mask is fabulous. Very lifelike. Can you breathe all right in there?'

'Stupid,' said Rose. 'I wish we had wolf days in my family too. Then I could go home now, just like Alfie in his stupid wolf suit.'

'Stop moaning, Rose,' Mr French said.

Alfie just nodded, then disappeared

quickly into the bushes before his teacher could ask him any more questions.

could ask him .... him.

39

What's that Noise?

Mr French shook his head as he watched them go. 'What a strange story! What a mega-strange story. But there's still one thing I don't get.' He turned around to Noura. 'Maybe you know, Noura. You were here before us. Who was the big, grey wolf Hunter Sam shot at? Is he part of Alfie's family too?'

Noura gave a big nod. 'That's a cousin of Alfie's, sir.'

Mr French looked at the trees thoughtfully. 'His wolf suit was fantastic too.

That horrible hunter almost shot the poor boy dead.'

Just then Hunter Sam groaned and moved a little.

'Come on, guys, it's time to head back now,' Mr French said.

'What about Hunter Sam?' asked Miss James.

'Leave him here. I've had more than enough of his company.'

Miss James nodded. 'Good idea. And what about that gun?'

'We'll take it with us! And accidentally lose it in a ditch on the way back. Does that sound like a good idea to you, Miss James?'

'An excellent idea, Mr French.'

Mr French sniggered. 'This time we're in complete agreement, Miss James.'

Suddenly he offered Miss James his arm. 'Those pancakes of yours really are excellent, did you know that? And I suspect you're quite good at football.'

Miss James just smiled, looking almost shy

186

as she slipped her arm through Mr French's.

'Come on, boys, girls, let's go.'

The teachers and children strode off.

'Look, there's the car!' Dad shouted. He was still wearing his wolf mask. Mum and Tim were carrying theirs under their arms.

Grandpa Werewolf laid a paw on Alfie's shoulder. 'You're in good hands, Alfie. Tim and his parents are crazy about you. They worry about you and they do their best to protect you. They're the best family you could ever hope for.'

Alfie nodded as they walked out from under the trees to where the car was parked on the edge of the forest. 'I know.'

'There's something else I wanted to ask you,' Grandpa Werewolf whispered. 'About that girl, Noura. I was wondering—'

That was as far as Grandpa got. Suddenly Alfie stopped and pricked up his ears. 'What's that noise?'

'What noise?' asked Tim.

'Listen.'

A quiet sobbing was coming from behind the car.

They hurried closer. Someone was sitting on the bumper, crying.

40

Teeth Marks

'Leo!' Alfie shouted. 'What's wrong?'

The big werewolf immediately burst in to more sobs.

'Leo be sad. Leo's ear be busted up. All smitherees. It hurtses, Leo's hurtsing like hellsbells. His ear be on fire.' He held his head in his two front paws.

Grandpa Werewolf walked up to him. 'Hush now, Leo. Let me have a look.'

'Ow, ow, it hurtses!' Leo screeched.

'Hmm, I see the problem,' Grandpa growled. 'You were lucky. The bullet only nicked your ear. There's just a teensy-weensy little bit missing.'

'Hurtsing,' Leo roared. 'Terriballistically hurtsing.'

Dad looked on, totally flabbergasted. He gave Alfie a gentle nudge. 'Um, who's that, Alfie?'

'Oh, that's Leo. Another one of Grandpa's grandsons. He's my cousin.'

'Hurtsing!' Leo sobbed. 'Leo's ear be brokened up!'

'Leave it to me,' Tim's mother said. 'Mums are dead good at things like this.' She grabbed the first aid kit out of the car, whipped out a bandage roll and started dressing Leo's ear. To finish off, she wrapped the bandage around his head like a turban. 'So, Leo, I bet it feels a lot better now.'

Leo beamed with pride. 'No hurtsing any more. Leo be happy.'

'See,' Mum said. 'There's a big boy.'

Leo looked at himself in the wing mirror. 'Cool!' he growled. 'Leo's got a handsome gobber.' He turned around to face the whole family, stood up straight and pounded his chest with his front paws. Then he looked up at the moon and let out a deafening howl, a bloodcurdling cry.

'Wow!' Dad whispered.

'Leo says byesie-bye now,' the big werewolf growled. 'Byesie-bye, little wolfie. Byesie-bye, Grandpa. Byesie-bye, big brother. Bye, Mumsy. Bye, Dadsy.' And with two enormous leaps, Leo disappeared into the trees.

'So,' Tim's father said, having taken off his wolf mask in the meantime. 'It's time for us to go home too. Are you coming with us, Grandpa?'

The old werewolf shook his head. 'No, not this time. I'm going after Leo, just to be on the safe side. He lives all alone in Sulphur Forest, you know. He has done for more than ten years.'

'All alone? The poor thing,' Mum said.

'Not at all,' Grandpa said. 'He's happy here. When he was seven he escaped from an orphanage. Then he found out that he was a werewolf, just like Alfie, and he never went back. He's lived here by himself ever since. I always look out for him, and that's what I'm going to do now.'

'You never told me I have a werewolf cousin,' Alfie said. Grandpa Werewolf grinned.

'There are lots of things I haven't told you, but you'll hear it all in good time.'

'Great,' Tim's father said, 'We'll see you next time then. I love werewolf secrets.' He waved and got into the car. Mum and Tim climbed in after him.

'Bye, Grandpa,' said Alfie.

'Um, one thing, Alfie,' Grandpa said. 'About that girl.'

Alfie looked at Grandpa with surprise. 'Noura?'

'Yes. I saw teeth marks on her neck,' Grandpa growled. 'There was even a little bit of blood. Did you do that? Did you bite her?'

Alfie nodded reluctantly. 'It was an accident, Grandpa. I was really happy. I didn't mean to bite her, it just happened.'

Grandpa Werewolf nodded thoughtfully. 'Hmm, then it can't be helped, I'm afraid.'

'Why? What do you mean, Grandpa?'

For a moment, Grandpa looked deep into Alfie's eyes. Then he shook his head. 'Nothing, son. Nothing to worry about. There's no use crying over spilt milk.'

Tim's father wound down the window. 'You coming, Alfie? We should get going.'

Alfie looked imploringly at Grandpa Werewolf. 'What do you mean, Grandpa? Tell me.'

Again Grandpa Werewolf shook his head. 'Don't worry, Alfie. Things happen the way they happen. Wait and see. Everything will become clear in time.'

'But . . .' Alfie started.

Grandpa Werewolf waved his walking stick, turned and walked in under the trees.

'See you next time, Alfie. Take care.'

Alfie watched his Grandpa until he too was swallowed up completely by the shadows. Then he got into the back of the car.

'So, off home again,' Dad exclaimed cheerfully. 'That's the end of our wolf day.'

41

Full Moon

In the night, Alfie shot up in bed, knowing immediately what had woken him. It was the third night of the full moon. Moonlight was shining on his bed and stroking his face.

Alfie stretched, then started scratching all over. His arms, his head, his legs. The werewolf itch got stronger. The moonlight got brighter and brighter. He felt hair growing on his cheeks. His ears started to stretch. His fingernails turned into claws.

Through the curtain, the moon shone into his room as Alfie scratched his hairy throat.

His hands had changed into wolf's paws. His face had changed into a wolf's muzzle.

He kicked off his duvet and jumped out of bed, quickly pulling off his pyjamas. Then he heard a quiet howling outside. Was it the howl of a wolf? Alfie's ears stood up. Wolves? Here? At home? Could it be Grandpa? Or Leo?

He walked over to the window and slid aside the curtain. The moon was as bright as a lamp that had been flicked on. The whole garden was bathed in light.

Sitting in that light, under Alfie's window, was a wolf. A small, pitch-black wolf, more or less the same size as Alfie.

'Huh?' growled Alfie. He opened his window and leant out with two paws on the window ledge. The black wolf was looking up at him. He knew those eyes! Brown eyes with golden speckles. A sudden chill seized him. All the hairs in his coat stood on end. His heart started pounding faster. And suddenly Alfie remembered Grandpa Werewolf's words.

'Wait and see,' Grandpa had said. 'Everything will become clear in time.'

Now Alfie understood! Noura! And Grandpa had known all along. Tears welled up in his eyes as he was overcome by powerless rage. Powerless sorrow.

'No!' he growled softly. 'No, no, no!'

42

Catch Me If You Can

The black wolf looked up silently.

Alfie peered down over the window ledge. 'I'm sorry, Noura,' he growled. 'It's my stupid fault. I accidentally bit you and now you're just like me.'

The black wolf didn't answer. She hates me, thought Alfie. She hates every rotten thing about me. Maybe she wants to rip me to shreds. But I still have to go to her. It's all my fault! I have to go down, no matter what happens. He climbed on to the window ledge. With one leap he was in the garden.

He sat down next to her. He had never felt so terrible in all his life.

'Are you really upset, Noura?'

The black wolf didn't answer. Alfie hung his head.

'I wish it hadn't happened. I really do!'

Alfie didn't dare to look at Noura. For a few seconds there was total silence. Suddenly he heard a soft snigger and looked up in surprise. The black wolf was looking at him and laughing. At least, that was what it sounded like.

'Are you laughing?' asked Alfie.

'You bet,' Noura replied. Then she snapped her teeth down hard on his ear. Alfie got the fright of his life.

'There, now we're even,' Noura growled. 'Catch me if you can.' She pushed Alfie over and raced off at top speed.

Stunned, Alfie scrambled to his feet. Noura had already leapt over the front fence.

'But, Noura, don't you think it's terrible? From now on, you'll be a werewolf like me. Every full moon you'll turn into a wolf.

Usually three nights in a row.'

Out in the middle of the road, Noura looked up at the moon and let out a cheerful howl.

'Don't be such a wet blanket, Alfie the Werewolf. I love it. And I bet I'm faster than you are.'

Alfie's heart leapt with joy. Noura was happy. Everything was OK. A big grin appeared on his face.

'Really?' he growled. 'You think you're faster? Just wait!' With one leap he was over the fence. 'Here I come, Noura!'

The black wolf was already at the end of the street.

'Noura, wait for me,' Alfie shouted. 'Shall we go out to dinner? It's on me. I know a fantastic henhouse. Right out on the other side of town.'

'Deal!' Noura called back.

She waited until Alfie had caught up to her, then the two young werewolves ran off down the street together, their shadows merging in the light of the full moon.